"I don't even know your last name."

"It's Langley."

He smiled at her. Those silky brown eyes held her prisoner.

"And yours?"

"Vaughn."

"It's nice to meet you, Eloise Vaughn."

"If I'm going out with you twelve times, then I'm getting twelve dates' worth of help."

"Deal."

She took in his handsome face. The fine lines that created his chiseled features. Those beautiful brown eyes.

A strange feeling worked its way through her. Real attraction.

Which would only wreck their deal and was the last thing in the world she wanted.

"This is where I draw the line. I'm fine walking myself upstairs."

With that she turned and strode into her building. She wouldn't risk being alone with him outside her apartment door when there was so much goodnight-kiss potential. She might be strong, but she wasn't perfect. She'd learned a long time ago that a smart woman didn't tempt fate.

Dear Reader

When I wrote DARING TO TRUST THE BOSS, I didn't begin with the idea of writing the stories of Olivia Prentiss's roommates. But I knew a single woman just starting out in a big, expensive city like New York City wouldn't be able to afford to live on her own, and her roommates were so vivid in the scenes in which they'd made an appearance that they made me curious! LOL!

Bored one day, I began doodling pasts for them, and Eloise Vaughn had such a rich backstory that I couldn't help wondering… Who would love her? Who would show her she was worth more than her wealthy parents believed when they kicked her out of their lives?

Enter Ricky Langley, also from DARING TO TRUST THE BOSS. A newly rich marketing genius, Ricky should be the happiest guy in the world—but there's a tragedy in his past…a tragedy for which he blames himself. He needs someone to love him for who he is, but also to bring him back to the real world.

They're a match made in heaven. Unfortunately they don't see it.

So how do you bring a woman to forget her sadness and a man to pretend—at least for a little while—that he has no troubles? You force them to go to twelve Christmas parties.

THE TWELVE DATES OF CHRISTMAS will always be one of my favourite books. Not just because it packs all the glitz and glamour a book can possibly cram into two hundred pages, but because it's a story of a true Christmas miracle—the story of two people finding real love.

I hope you enjoy it! (And, oh, by the way…wait until you see what I've cooked up for sweet, unsuspecting Laura Beth Matthews!)

Merry Christmas!

Susan Meier

THE
TWELVE DATES
OF CHRISTMAS

BY
SUSAN MEIER

Published in Great Britain 2014
by Mills & Boon, an imprint of Harlequin (UK) Limited,
Eton House, 18-24 Paradise Road, Richmond, Surrey, TW9 1SR

© 2014 Linda Susan Meier

ISBN: 978-0-263-24334-5

Susan Meier spent most of her twenties thinking she was a job-hopper—until she began to write and realised everything that had come before was only research! One of eleven children, with twenty-four nieces and nephews and three kids of her own, Susan has had plenty of real-life experience watching romance blossom in unexpected ways. She lives in western Pennsylvania with her wonderful husband, Mike, three children, and two overfed, well-cuddled cats, Sophie and Fluffy. You can visit Susan's website at: www.susanmeier.com

Recent books by Susan Meier:

DARING TO TRUST THE BOSS
SINGLE DAD'S CHRISTMAS MIRACLE
A FATHER FOR HER TRIPLETS**
HER PREGNANCY SURPRISE
THE BILLIONAIRE'S BABY SOS†
NANNY FOR THE MILLIONAIRE'S TWINS*
THE TYCOON'S SECRET DAUGHTER*
KISSES ON HER CHRISTMAS LIST

**Mothers in a Million*
†Part of *The Larkville Legacy*
First Time Dads! duet

This and other titles by Susan Meier are available in eBook format from www.millsandboon.co.uk

DEDICATION

For my sisters…
May we always take care of each other
the way Olivia, Eloise and Laura Beth do.

CHAPTER ONE

THERE WAS ALWAYS too much month left at the end of Eloise Vaughn's money.

"Here, put these crackers in your purse." Laura Beth Matthews gathered a handful of crackers from the party buffet of their newly married friend, Olivia Engle, and shoved them at Eloise.

She gasped. "So now we're reduced to stealing crackers?"

"Five crackers are lunch."

Eloise sighed but opened her Chanel purse and let her roommate dump the crackers inside.

"I'm sorry, Coco."

Laura Beth said, "Coco?"

"Chanel…" She shook her head. "Never mind."

Hoping no one saw the crackers falling into her purse, Eloise glanced around the Christmas party at the women wearing shiny cocktail dresses in shades of red and green and the tuxedo-clad men. Subdued gold and silver decorations gave the Engles' penthouse a sophisticated glow. The clink of ice in glasses, laughter of guests and the air of importance—wealth and power—wafted around her.

For fifty cents she could work this room and probably leave with a date. But she didn't want a date. She'd had the love of her life and had lost him. Now, she wanted a job, a good-paying job, a permanent position that would support her. Unfortunately, her degree didn't seem to translate well into actual work. In lieu of a job, she'd take another roommate, someone to help with the rent on the apartment she shared with Laura Beth. Then the pressure would be off, and the salary from the temp job she currently had at a law firm would be enough that she and Laura Beth could buy food again.

But she wouldn't find a roommate here. All of these people could afford their own condos. Maybe two condos...and a beach house.

Laura Beth studied the remaining food. "It's too bad we can't pour some of this dip in our purses."

Eloise shoved her purse behind her back. "I draw the line at dip. No dip. Not on the inside of my Chanel."

"You do realize you could sell some of those overpriced clothes, handbags and shoes you own and probably eat for an entire year."

"Most of my stuff is five years old. No one would want it."

Laura Beth sniffed a laugh. "You make it work."

"Only because I know how to change a collar or add a belt."

"So update your stuff and then sell it."

She couldn't. Not that she loved clothes and dressing up so much that she'd die without accessories. It was more that these clothes were the last piece of herself she had. The last piece of the starry-eyed college junior, one year away from graduating, who'd run away and married her Prince Charming.

Her heart pinched. Prince Charming seemed like an odd description. Especially given that she and Wayne had had their troubles. After they married, her wealthy parents had disowned her, and Wayne couldn't find a job. So she'd had to work as a waitress, and they'd fought. A lot. Then he'd been diagnosed with pancreatic cancer, and in what seemed like the blink of an eye, he'd died. Overwhelmed with grief and confused that death could be so swift and so cruel, she'd gone home, hoping her parents would help her cope. But they wouldn't even come to the door. Through the maid, they'd reminded her that they had disowned her and didn't want her and her troubles visiting their doorstep.

At first she'd been crushed, then she was sad, then she got angry. But that only fueled her determination. Come hell or high water she intended to make it. Big. She didn't know where or how, but she intended to make it. Not just to show her parents, but so she could be happy again.

"I'd like you to meet my cousin."

Ricky Langley glanced up in horror as his lawyer walked up to him with a thirty-something woman. With her hair in a tight black ball on the back of her head and her bright red dress clinging to her curves, she eyed him appreciatively.

"Janine Barron, this is Ricky Langley."

"It's a pleasure." Her voice shivered just the tiniest bit, as if she were so thrilled to meet him she couldn't quite catch her breath.

Another man might have been pleased—maybe even proud—that his lawyer liked him enough to introduce him to a relative. But since his son had died, he'd been besieged by a loss so intense that thoughts of love, romance or even meeting somebody weren't anywhere on his radar.

He said, "It's nice to meet you," and managed ten minutes of polite conversation, but when he found an opportunity, he slipped away.

He wove through conversation groups as he walked across Tucker Engle's sleek living room. Although Tucker had married six months ago, his New York City penthouse still claimed the sophisticated furnishings of a bachelor pad. Chrome and black leather furniture sat on white shag carpet atop dark hardwood floors. The Christmas tree Tucker had decorated with his new wife, Olivia, glittered with all silver and gold ornaments. The cherrywood mantel over the fireplace boasted one stocking...for Baby Engle. Not yet born, the child hadn't been named. They wouldn't tell the sex either. It was all to be a grand surprise.

He pursed his lips as his breathing stuttered. He thought of the one and only Christmas he'd shared with his son. Blake had been born December twenty-seventh, so he was two days shy of a year on his first Christmas day. He'd clapped when he'd seen the tree lit with brightly colored lights that reflected off the tinsel. He'd eaten Christmas cookies. And he'd gone just a bit bananas when he'd awakened Christmas morning to find tons of gifts all for him. He couldn't talk, so he squeaked and squealed for joy. He had torn off wrapping paper, liked the boxes better than the actual gifts and in general made a mess of Ricky's pristine penthouse.

It had been the best Christmas of Ricky's life. And now he had nothing.

He sucked in a breath. He shouldn't have come to this party. He might be eighteen months into his grief, but some things, like Christmas celebrations, would always level him. Worse, he had twelve more of these events on his calendar. Ten parties, one wedding and one fraternity reunion. Last year, six months into his grief, he could reasonably bow out. This year, people were beginning to worry.

He turned to race away from the mantle and bumped into somebody's purse. He swore he heard a crunch as his hands swung around to catch his victim.

"Damn it! I think you crushed my crackers."

The scowl on the blonde's beautiful face surprised him so much he forgot he was too unhappy to talk with anyone. "You have crackers in your purse?"

She sighed heavily and tucked a strand of her long yellow hair behind her ear. "Not usually." She glanced at his tuxedo, gave him a quick once-over, then shook her head. "Never mind. You're a little too rich to understand."

"Oh, you took crackers from the buffet table for lunch next week." At her horrified look, he inclined his head. "I used to be poor. Did the same thing at parties."

"Yeah, well, this was my roommate's idea. Typically, I'm not the kind of girl who steals."

"You're not stealing. Those crackers were set out for the guests. You're a guest. Besides, it's the end of the night. Once we all leave, the leftovers will probably be thrown away. Or given to a homeless shelter."

She squeezed her eyes shut in misery. "Great. Now I'm taking crackers out of the mouths of homeless people. I hate this city."

He gaped at her. "How can you hate New York?"

"I don't hate New York, per se. I just hate that it costs so much to live here."

She suddenly straightened. Right before his eyes she changed from a frantic working girl into a princess.

Her shoulders back, her smile polite and subdued, she said, "If you'll excuse me, I want to say goodbye to Olivia and Tucker."

He stepped out of her way. "Of course."

Three things hit him at once. First, she was gorgeous. Her gold dress hugged her high breasts, slim waist and round bottom as if it were made for her. Second, she was refined and polite for someone reduced to taking the extra crackers from a party. Third, she'd barely given him a second look.

"Ricky!"

Ricky pivoted and saw his attorney scrambling toward him.

"I understand your reluctance to get back into the swing of things, but I'm not going to apologize for trying to find you someone. If you don't soon start dating, people are going to wonder about you."

Hadn't he just thought the same thing himself? "I hope they come up with some good stories."

"This isn't funny. You're a businessman. People don't want to sign contracts with unstable men."

"Being single doesn't make me unstable. I can name lots of men who did very well as bachelors."

"Yeah, but most of them don't have a children's video game line they're about to release."

He turned away. "I'll take my chances."

His attorney caught his arm and stopped him. "You'll be wrong. Look, do you want support when you take this new company public next year? Then you'd better look alive. Like a guy worth supporting."

His attorney stormed off at the same time Cracker Girl walked by, her head twisting from side to side as if she were looking for someone.

A starburst of pleasure shot through him, surprising him. She *was* beautiful. Physically perfect. And with a conscience. Although taking crackers from a party didn't rank up there with grand theft auto, he could see it upset her.

He laughed and shook his head, but he stopped midmotion. Good grief. She'd made him laugh.

With the party officially winding down, Eloise retrieved her black wool cape, a classic that never went out of style. By the time she reached the elevator, Tucker and Olivia were already there, saying goodbye to guests.

The plush little car took the couple in front of her away. She smiled at Olivia and caught her hands. "It was a wonderful party."

Pregnant and glowing with it, blond-haired, blue-eyed Olivia said, "Thanks."

"It was great seeing your parents too. Where did they run off to? I tried to find them to say goodbye but they were gone."

"Dad wanted to be in bed early so he and Mom could get up early. We're all going to Kentucky tomorrow."

"Celebrating Christmas from the last Friday in November to January second," Tucker said with a laugh.

"You're taking more than a month off?"

"Yes!" Olivia joyfully said. "Five weeks! We're coming back for one party mid-December, but other than that we'll be in Kentucky."

Eloise smiled. She'd wondered why Tucker and Olivia had had their Christmas party so early.

"It's going to be such fun. We'll sleigh ride and skate." She smiled at her handsome husband, a dark-haired, thirty-something former confirmed bachelor she'd fallen in love with in Italy. "And drink hot chocolate by the fire."

"Sounds perfect." *For Olivia.* The woman lived and breathed the fairy tale. But Eloise wanted a real life. With her husband dead and most of the magic sucked out of life, all she wanted to be was normal, to get a job and *never* depend on anyone but herself again.

She glanced around. "Have you seen Laura Beth?"

Olivia caught Eloise's hand and pulled her to the side. "She left ten minutes ago with one of Tucker's vice presidents."

Eloise's chest tightened. "Really?"

"They were talking stock options and market fluctuations when they said goodbye to us. I overheard them saying something about going to a coffee shop."

"Oh."

"Do you need a taxi?"

She licked her suddenly dry lips. A taxi? Obviously Olivia had forgotten how much a taxi cost. The plan had been for her and Laura Beth to take the subway. Together. She didn't want to ride alone this late at night and couldn't believe Laura Beth had ditched her.

Still, that wasn't Olivia's problem. If anything, Eloise and Laura Beth had vowed to keep their financial distress from their now-wealthy friend so she wouldn't do something kind, but awkward, like pay their rent.

"Um. No. I don't need a taxi." She smiled. "I'm taking the subway."

"Alone?"

"I love the subway." That wasn't really a lie. She did love the subway. It was cheap and efficient. But at night, alone, it was also scary.

"Oh, Eloise! I don't want you to risk it. Let Tucker call his driver."

"We're fine."

"*You're* alone."

Drat. She'd hoped Olivia wouldn't notice that tricky maneuvering use of "we" to make her think she had company for the subway.

Tucker caught Olivia's hand to get her attention. "Ricky's leaving."

Eloise turned to see the guy who had tried to tell her stealing crackers was okay. He had dark hair and dark eyes, and he looked amazing in a tux. Sexy.

She sucked in a breath. Noticing he was sexy had been an accident. She refused to notice any guy until she was financially stable.

Olivia stood on tiptoes and kissed his cheek.

All right. He was tall. It was hard not to notice someone was tall.

He straightened away from Olivia, and Eloise frowned. It was also hard not to notice smooth, sexy brown eyes that had a sleepy, smoldering way of looking at a woman. And that hair? Dark. Shaggy. So out of style she should want to walk him to a hair salon. Instead, she was tempted to brush it off his forehead.

Wow. Seriously? What was wrong with her? She had not intended to take note of any of that. But the guy was simply too gorgeous not to notice.

"Good night, Ricky. Thanks for coming to the party. I hope you enjoyed it."

"It was great."

He kissed Olivia's cheek, and Eloise stood there like an idiot, realizing her mistake. When he'd walked over, she should have taken advantage of Olivia's preoccupation and slipped into the elevator. Nothing was worse than the guilt of a former roommate who hadn't just found the love of her life but also her calling. While Eloise and Laura Beth floundered, Olivia had hit the life lottery and was married, pregnant and a manager for young artists. And now she couldn't stop worrying about her former roommates.

Eloise didn't want to be anybody's burden. She was smart, educated. With the right job, she could be happy as a clam. It was finding that job that seemed impossible. Until she did, she'd be poor. And Olivia would worry.

Olivia glanced at Eloise and, as if just seeing the obvious, she gasped. "You've met Eloise, right?"

The guy named Ricky looked over at her. "I bumped into her by the fireplace."

"She's on her way home, but her friend left early." Olivia winced. "Talking business with one of Tucker's employees."

Eloise supposed she shouldn't be angry because that might lead to a better job for Laura Beth, but she knew the next words coming out of Olivia's mouth before she even heard them.

"You have your limo, right?" She put her hand on her tummy, looking beautiful and Madonna like, the kind of woman no man could refuse. "You wouldn't mind taking Eloise to her apartment, would you?"

Eloise immediately said, "No. I'm fine."

At the same time, Ricky said, "Actually, I think I owe her a favor."

Olivia beamed. "Great."

The elevator doors swished open.

Ricky smiled at her and motioned to the door. "After you."

She stepped inside. As the doors closed, she waved to Olivia. "Thanks again for inviting me."

Tucker and Olivia waved back, looking like the perfect couple. "Thanks for coming."

The doors met and the little car began its descent.

"So...your friend dumped you."

"We're both trying to find jobs that pay better than what we have so we can afford our rent. She was talking business with one of Tucker's executives. I can't fault her for that."

"How long have you been in New York?"

"Three years."

"That's a long time to still be scraping by."

"We were fine until Olivia left us."

Even though she had a good excuse for her poverty, embarrassment rumbled through her. She might have been born into money, but she'd gone to the school of hard knocks. Paid her dues. Gotten her education in spite of her grief and confusion. Now all she wanted was a job.

Was that really so much to ask?

Ricky waited in silence as the elevator descended. From the tension crackling off Eloise Whatever-Her-Last-Name-Was, he could tell she wasn't happy that he was taking her home. Actually, he could tell she wasn't happy period. Her financial situation was abysmal. Her friend Olivia was living a great life. Her other friend had deserted her.

She had a lot of pride. Which he couldn't argue. He had a bit of pride himself. But he wasn't going to let a pretty single girl ride the subway alone after midnight. Especially not one who had made him laugh.

The elevator door opened and she sped out into the frosty cold night. He ambled behind her. When she reached the sidewalk, she stopped dramatically.

He wasn't the only one who had called for his limo. Four

long black cars sat in a cluster in front of the building. No way for her to pass. No way for her to hail a cab.

He paused behind her, slid his arm around her shoulders and pointed at the third one down. His fingers accidentally brushed the back of her neck, and the tips tingled at the feeling of her soft, soft skin.

He cleared his throat. "I'm number three. Just accept a ride."

She straightened regally. "All right."

When they reached his car, Norman, his driver, opened the door. She slid inside. He slid in beside her. A minute later, Norman's door closed and the engine hummed to life.

"Wanna give me your address so I can tell the driver where to take you?"

She told him, then sat staring at her coat while he used the internal intercom system to inform Norman.

The next five minutes passed in silence. Finally, unable to bear her misery anymore, he said, "I really was as poor as you when I moved to the city. I don't mind taking you home. This isn't an imposition. It isn't charity. It's a happy coincidence that we were leaving at the same time. Please, stop feeling bad."

To his surprise, she turned on him. "Feeling bad? I don't feel bad! I'm mad. I'm sick of people pitying me when all I want is a decent job. I'm educated enough to get one, but no one seems to want me."

"What's your degree in?"

"Human resources."

"Ouch. You know human resources functions can be folded into administration or accounting. And that's exactly what happens in a recession."

"I know. Lucky me."

She had enough pride to fill an ocean. But she also had a weird sense of humor about it. Enough that he'd almost laughed again. Twice. In one night. Both times because of her.

"Now, don't get snooty. Surely, there are other things you can do."

"I've waitressed, and apparently a degree can also get you a lot of temporary secretarial work because right now I'm in a six-week gig at a law firm."

"That's something."

She sighed tiredly. "Actually, it is. I don't mean to sound ungrateful. I know others have it a lot worse."

He was one of those people who had it worse than she did. But he didn't share that—not even with people who almost made him laugh. She'd go from treating him normally to feeling sorry for him. And for once, just once, he wanted to be with somebody who didn't feel sorry for him.

He glanced at the floor and was nearly struck blind by the glitter of her shoes. His gazed traveled up her trim legs to the black cape she wore. Her shiny gold dress peeked above the coat's collar.

For a struggling woman, she dressed very well. Of course, her clothes could be old. Or she could have gotten them from a secondhand store.

But even if she'd gotten them from a thrift store, she'd known what to choose and how to wear it. Actually, if he thought about it, she had the look of every socialite he'd been introduced to in the past year.

Except she wasn't one. She didn't have any money.

"What Laura Beth and I really need is another roommate."

He spared her a glance. "That shouldn't be too hard to find."

"Huh! We've tried. We never seem to pick someone who fits with us."

He turned on the seat. "Really? Why?"

"The first girl we let in had a record we didn't know about until her parole officer called."

He chuckled, amazed that she'd done it again. So easily, so effortlessly, she could make him laugh. "I dated somebody like that once. Turned out abysmally."

"Yeah, well, Judy took my coffeemaker when she left."

"Ouch."

"The references for the second one were faked."

"You need Jason Jones."

"Excuse me?"

"That's the search engine I created. Well, I came up with the idea. Elias Greene actually wrote the programs. It investigates people."

"Really?"

"Yeah. It's great. It'll tell you things you never even realized you wanted to know." He smiled politely. "I'd let you use it for free."

She squeezed her eyes shut in distress. "I don't want your handouts. I don't want anybody's handouts!"

Yeah. He could see that. He didn't know where she'd come from, but she had guts and grit. She wanted to make it on her own.

"We could bargain for it."

She gasped and scrambled away from him. "Not on your life."

He laughed. Again. Fourth time. "I'm not talking about sex."

She relaxed but gave him a strange look. "I don't have anything to bargain." She petted her coat. "Unless you're into vintage women's clothes."

"Nope. But you do have something I want."

Her gazed strolled over to his cautiously, wary. "What?"

"Time."

"Time?"

"Yeah. I have ten Christmas parties, a wedding and a fraternity reunion coming up. I need a date."

CHAPTER TWO

ELOISE STARED AT Ricky Whatever. "I don't even know your last name."

"It's Langley." He smiled at her. Those silky brown eyes held her prisoner. "And yours?"

"Vaughn."

He reached out and shook her hand. "It's nice to meet you, Eloise Vaughn."

"So you have twelve places to go for Christmas and you want me to go out with you?"

"No. I want you to be my date. Big difference."

She eyed him askance. "I'm not sure how."

"There'd be nothing romantic between us." He winced. "Except to pretend that there is. I need space. A reason to bow out of conversations. Bringing a date to parties has a way of giving a guy options."

She studied him, realized he was serious and said the thing he was dancing around but wouldn't quite say. "And you want people to stop fixing you up all the time. With someone at your side, they'd leave you alone."

"It's more complicated than that. Really what it comes down to is easing myself back into the world and into my social circle. A date at my side would be like a living symbol to my friends that I'm fine, and they can all stop worrying about me."

Eloise got comfortable against the supple leather seat. He talked like a guy coming off a bad relationship. Nobody wanted to have to go to parties when they were smarting from a breakup. He probably didn't want to have to explain where his ex was. Or, worse, have to flirt or be flirted with.

"So you're looking for ways to be able to go to parties without being social."

"I don't mind being social. I just don't want to have to be too social. Look, I'm not in the market for something romantic, so you'd be perfectly safe. You might even enjoy yourself. Meet some new people. Make some work contacts."

Yep. Anybody who wasn't in the market for something romantic was still hurting over a bad breakup. But he'd also said the magic words. Work contacts. The employment market was so tight she couldn't even get interviews. But if she could meet the higher-ups of some companies, she might impress them and maybe open a door for herself.

"And I don't have to do anything but smile and be polite?"

"And pretend to like me."

She already sort of liked him. He was handsome and just a little bit scruffy, the way a man was when there was no woman in his life. And he was honest. So pretending to like him wouldn't be hard.

"We'd need a story."

"A story?"

"How we met. Why we're dating."

"Why don't we just say we met at Olivia and Tucker's party and hit it off?"

"It's only half a lie. We did meet at the party. But we didn't exactly hit it off. We barely spoke."

"We're talking like two friends now."

She thought about that. "Yeah. I guess we are." She sucked in a breath. "And you'd help me find a job?"

"You don't want to use Jason Jones to find a roommate?"

"A roommate is temporary. I want a permanent solution. I want a career."

His brow wrinkled. "Are you asking me to hire you?"

She gaped at him. "God, no! I don't want to be the girl in the office who got her job by dating the boss. Sheesh! Talk about instant pariah. I want you to get me job with one of your friends."

"I can't get you *hired*, but I could help you make contacts."

She shook her head. "If I'm going out with you—" She did the math in her head…ten parties, one wedding, one fraternity reunion "—twelve times, then I'm getting twelve dates' worth of help."

"What do you want me to do? Run an ad saying that someone should hire you?"

"I don't care what you do. Pick your friends' brains to see who's looking for an HR person and get me interviews, and I'll go out with you *twelve*," she deliberately exaggerated the word so he'd see the significance of the big number, "times."

His eyes told her he was doing a bit of mental calculating—proving he took her seriously—before he stuck out his hand to shake hers. "Deal."

She took it. "Deal."

They reached her apartment building. She slid out of the limo, and he did too. "You don't have to walk me upstairs."

"Someone could be hiding—"

She put her hand on his chest and was surprised that she met a solid wall. He was a lot stronger than he looked. Probably all muscle under that trim tux.

Now that they were going to spend a lot of time together, that meant something. She took in his handsome face. The fine lines that created his chiseled features. Those beautiful brown eyes.

A strange feeling worked its way through her. It took a second to recognize it, but it was attraction. Real attraction. Not just the I-think-he's-handsome feeling. But more like the I-could-sleep-with-him-someday feeling.

Which would only wreck their deal and was the last thing in the world she wanted. She'd gone the route of love. Now she realized having a job was a more secure happily-ever-after. Plus, he'd said he wasn't interested in anything romantic. She couldn't be either.

She removed her hand. "This is where I draw the line. I'm fine walking myself upstairs. And you need to believe me."

"But—"

"No." With that she turned and strode into her building. He was handsome, but neither of them was in the market for a romance. And she needed their deal. She hadn't been able to make job inroads for herself. He might be able to help her. She wouldn't risk being alone with him outside her apartment door when there was so much goodnight-kiss potential. She might be strong, but she wasn't perfect. She'd learned a long time ago that a smart woman didn't tempt fate.

The next morning she woke confused. Or maybe disoriented. She hadn't gotten drunk, so she didn't have a hangover. But that meant she also didn't have an excuse for agreeing to go on twelve dates with a stranger.

Although he wasn't really a stranger. He was a friend of Olivia and Tucker's. Someone Olivia liked enough that she'd gone up on tiptoes to kiss his cheek. Olivia would have the scoop on him.

She grabbed her phone from the bedside table and headed for the kitchen. After throwing together a pot of coffee in an old drip coffeemaker instead of her sleek one-cup one stolen by Judy, she speed dialed Olivia.

"Hi, this is Olivia Engle. You've reached my voice mail. Please leave a message after the beep."

Drat. She'd forgotten Olivia and her family were leaving early for Kentucky. She wouldn't have her phone on. Heck, she might not turn on her phone for the entire month of December. What had she said? She and Tucker would be having family time?

She tossed her phone to the table before she sat. So much for asking Olivia about Ricky Langley.

Laura Beth trudged into the kitchen. Her long brown hair lay in disarray on her shoulders. Her green eyes were barely open. "Who were you calling?"

"Olivia. I needed some insider information, but then I remembered she's flying to Kentucky today."

Reaching into the cupboard for a cup and a tea bag, Laura Beth asked, "What kind of insider information?"

"A little background on a guy. I think I may have found a way to get a job."

Laura Beth's eyes widened. "Really?"

"Yes. And, by the way, thanks for deserting me last night."

"Sorry. Bruce heads Tucker's newly created IT department. I went for coffee and got an interview."

"Yeah, well, the guy I met last night wants a date for some parties."

"Oh my God, you're not—" Her eyes grew as big as two dinner plates and she couldn't finish.

"Not *that* kind of date. Ricky Langley seems to be coming off a big breakup, and he doesn't want to go to his Christmas social engagements alone. So he asked me to go to all his parties. In exchange, he'll introduce me to influential people and pick their brains about job openings."

"That sounds almost as promising as my job interview. Maybe more promising because you could get a couple of prospects."

The comment eased away the little bit of confusion Eloise had had about this deal. Ricky was Olivia and Tucker's friend. He hadn't made a pass. He'd made a deal. She liked deals. She liked giving something to get something. She absolutely hated charity.

So she'd try this, giving him one date to prove himself. And if he didn't, she'd end it.

This did not have to be something to stress over.

He called around ten o'clock, apologetic because the first party he needed her to attend with him was that night.

"Already? It won't even be December for two days."

"My friends start early." He paused, then said, "Is that a problem?"

"No. It's fine. It might be Saturday, but I don't date and I don't have enough money to go out myself." She winced, realizing how pathetic she sounded. "I meant that to be reassuring, not whiny."

"Yeah. I got it."

"So what time will you pick me up?"

"Around eight." He hesitated, not sounding any more sure of this weird arrangement than she was, then added, "This party is being thrown by my banker."

"Any idea how I should dress?"

"I think the same way you did for Tucker and Olivia's party." He paused. "You looked nice."

The simple compliment gave her far too much pleasure. She shook it off. "Thanks. But that was a cocktail dress. If this event is formal, I may need to wear a gown."

"It's black tie at the Waldorf."

"I'm wearing a gown."

"Fine. But don't be waiting in the lobby of your building. Let me come up. I don't want my driver telling his other driver buddies that I make my dates meet me on the street."

She hadn't wanted them to get too personal, but the whole point was for this to look real. He was right; it would be odd if she was waiting for him in her building lobby. "Okay."

She headed back to her bedroom to find something to wear. With twelve cocktail dresses, several ball gowns and just about anything he needed her to wear for any occasion, she had plenty of possibilities. Except everything she owned was out of style.

She pulled a red gown from the rack. She would think bankers would like red… No. No. Green. Like money. With a laugh, she reached for a green velvet gown. It would need tons of updating, but she didn't care. In the past few years, she'd developed a way with scissors and a needle and thread. She'd gotten so good at refurbishing old clothes that she'd actually bought a secondhand sewing machine so she could make real alterations.

Smiling as she went in search of her scissors, she realized she was really looking forward to going out. She would meet people in a position to hire her. But also she had a reason to dress up. To socialize. Maybe even dance. It would be fun.

She couldn't remember the last time she'd had fun.

As long as Ricky Langley really was a gentleman, this arrangement could be good for a bundle of reasons.

He arrived a little before eight. Still excited, she opened the door, and her eyes widened. She'd forgotten how good-looking he was. Dressed in a tux with a black top coat, he was so gorgeous, so sophisticated, he could have been the king of a small country.

She quickly pulled herself together. His amazingness did not matter. She did not want to be attracted to anybody. She wanted a job.

"Let me get my coat."

Nodding, he strolled into her apartment, but she didn't give him a lot of time to look around. It wasn't that she was ashamed of her living space. Actually, she was proud of the fact that she had come as far as she had with absolutely no help. But she was eager to get out the door and go to a party. In a pretty gown. Something she'd made even prettier.

She flipped her cape over her back and walked toward him.

"You look incredible."

Pride sizzled through her. He wouldn't have said that if he'd seen this dress five hours ago. "Thanks. I loved this dress when I bought it." They walked to the door, and she closed it behind them. "So it was fantastic to have a reason to bring it up to date."

She led the way down the stairs.

"You updated your dress?"

"Yes. I took off the collar and the belt and did a little something to the back."

"Oh."

She glanced over her shoulder at him. "You don't have to worry that I'm going to embarrass you. I don't have money to buy new things, but I have plenty of old things I can fix or update. And I've gotten very good with a sewing machine. No one will even notice that this dress used to look totally different."

The conversation died, and they stayed silent on the drive to the Waldorf. The building façade had been covered in white lights, which were also woven through the branches of the fir trees standing like sentinels on both side of the entryway.

Memories of the time she'd come here with her parents flooded her. It had been her first formal party, and she was so nervous at meeting her dad's friends and business associates that she'd sworn real butterflies were in her tummy.

Mind your manners.
Don't speak unless spoken to.

You are a guest. The daughter of a wealthy man. Your comportment should say that.

The doorman came over and opened the door of Ricky's limo.

She drew in a breath and let him help her out. That's when she saw the other attendees. Furs. Diamonds. Hair coiffed to perfection.

She slid her hand down her cape, which looked foolish compared to the furs being worn by the other women exiting limos, and turned to Ricky. "I'm guessing the guy knows a few wealthy people."

He smiled, motioning for her to walk under the portico and to the steps leading to the hotel. "Expect a camera or two on the way in. A photographer for the society pages will take a shot of everyone in the hope of getting something for tomorrow's paper."

She faltered. "Oh." Her mother might live in Kentucky, but she got all the New York papers so she could "keep up" with her own kind. She lived and breathed the society pages.

Fear shimmied along her nerve endings. She couldn't seem to make her feet move. She hadn't seen her parents in five years. Not since they'd disowned her. But if they saw her at a society event with a wealthy man, God only knew what they'd do. Happy she'd finally come to her senses, would they call her? Pretend nothing had happened? And if they did, what would she do? Was she lonely enough, desperate enough, to pretend it was okay that they hadn't cared that her husband had died and that she was struggling to get her bearings?

She squeezed her eyes shut. Why hadn't she thought of this?

Ricky's voice came to her slowly, softly. "You don't mind getting your picture taken, do you?"

She popped her eyes open. "It depends on where it will end up."

He took her elbow and guided her up the steps to the entryway. "Probably nowhere. We'd have to be important enough for a society columnist to want to comment on us."

"And you're not important?"

Another uniformed hotel employee opened the door and they walked inside. "Last year I was everybody's charity case. This year, I'm nothing. You're safe."

Relief poured through her, but it was short-lived. Not only was she in a dress from five years ago, updated by collar-and-belt removal, but also no one could predict who a society columnist might deem important to write about. If Ricky Langley hadn't dated anybody in a year, his suddenly appearing with a woman might spark curiosity.

As they walked through the ornate lobby, she saw a camera raised toward her, and as smoothly as possible, she ducked behind Ricky.

He turned. "What are you doing?"

"Oh, I just thought because you have the invitation, you should go first."

He frowned. "The lobby is wide enough that we can walk side by side."

Seeing the photographer's attention had been caught by another guest, she laughed. "Of course. I'm sorry."

They entered the elevator and rode up to the ballroom in silence. Ricky noticed that she'd kept hugging her cape, almost as if she was trying to hide it, and winced a bit internally. She clearly believed she didn't belong here and was embarrassed.

But wariness overcame his worry. This was their first date. He wanted her to have a good time and meet perspective employers, but he was more concerned with how his friends reacted to *her*. If they didn't believe their dating was real, then all bets were off, and she wouldn't have to worry about how she looked.

The doors opened, and they walked out of the elevator together.

He caught her gaze. "Let me take your cape for coat check."

She slid it off and handed it to him. He shrugged out of his top coat and gave the two to the young woman manning the station.

They turned to go into the dimly lit foyer that would take them to the ballroom, and a photographer snapped their picture. Eloise's face drained of color. He would've sworn she swayed.

At Tucker and Olivia's party, she'd given him the impression she was as close to a princess as a woman could be without actually being royalty. Yet she was suddenly shaking in her shoes.

"Are you okay?"

She faced him with an overbright smile. "Yeah. Sure. I'm fine."

He knew she wasn't. Her eyes shone with fear. Her face was pasty white.

"You're not afraid to meet these people, are you?"

She sucked in a breath. "I need to meet these people."

"So what's wrong?"

"I hate to have my picture taken."

Which explained all the questions she'd had about the photographers...but raised new ones about why she wouldn't want her picture taken.

Before he could say anything, regal Eloise reappeared. She straightened to her full height. Her expression shifted. The green dress that she'd altered slid along her curves like decadence incarnate. She turned and headed for the entrance to the ballroom, and Ricky's eyes bulged.

The neckline might be normal in the front, but the back dipped to the bottom of her spine. Smooth yellow hair flirted with her naked skin, swishing back and forth.

His mouth watered.

How the hell had he missed that her dress had virtually no back?

Realizing he wasn't following her, she stopped and faced him. "Do you like getting your picture taken by people you don't know?"

He raced to catch up with her. "I've been getting my picture taken by strangers for so long I guess it doesn't faze me anymore. Especially because they rarely turn up anywhere."

She shook her mane of yellow hair down her back and strode ahead again. "Fine."

Watching her walk away, he stood frozen. The smooth material of her dress caressed her perfect butt so well the fact that she didn't like getting her picture taken faded into insignificance. At Tucker and Olivia's he'd noticed she was gorgeous, but in that dress she was a showstopper.

Which was perfect. One look at her and everybody would totally understand why he had come out of his self-imposed social hiatus and was going out with her.

Imagining his friends' reactions to her, he bit back a cheesy grin and caught up to her right before the desk where he'd present his invitation. There could be a million reasons why she didn't like getting her picture taken, and most of them were innocent. He wasn't going to ruin what could be the perfect return to the party scene with unfounded suspicions.

"If it's any consolation, cameras are off-limits in the party."

"Yes. It is a consolation."

He presented his invitation at the discreet desk by the entry, and they were routed to the greeting line for the host and hostess.

Paul Montgomery's eyes lit when he saw Eloise. "My darling, however did you get this guy to finally break down and bring a date somewhere?"

She laughed and slid her arm through Ricky's. "We met at the party of a mutual friend."

"Tucker and Olivia Engle," Ricky said, shaking the old

man's hand. "She's a friend of Olivia's. I'm a friend of Tucker's."

"Oh, we love Olivia," Mrs. Paul Montgomery said, leaning in to air kiss Eloise's cheek. "She simply glows with her pregnancy."

Eloise smiled. "She certainly does. She will make an amazing mother."

Their twenty seconds of greeting time expended, Ricky and Eloise were guided to the next section, where they were given their table number and a hand-carved Christmas ornament as a gift from the Montgomerys.

The huge ballroom shimmered with laughing, talking people. Rich red velvet drapes billowed from ceiling-high windows and glittered festively as if they'd been sprinkled with stardust. Round tables boasted gold tablecloths and huge centerpieces of calla lilies and evergreens accented by a ribbon of gold that wove through them.

Ricky took Eloise's hand and guided her through the sea of round tables. "That went smoothly."

"Our story's very believable."

"Then we'll stick with it." He paused, turned and caught her gaze. Now that he'd realized the impact gorgeous Eloise would make on his friends, a bit of fear tugged at his gut.

"We're seated with some of my best friends. I don't want them to know you're a fake date. These are the people I most want to reassure that I'm fine. Dating someone is the living, breathing symbol of that. If we're convincing enough, they won't ask questions. They'll see I'm fine."

"Okay."

"But if anybody even suspects you're a fake date, I'm going to look pathetic. This has to be as real as possible for my friends to buy in. That means I'm going to put my arm around you."

She nodded.

He sucked in a breath. "And we're going to dance because I love to dance, and it will look odd if I bring a date and don't dance."

She straightened the collar of his tux, then tightened his bow tie, the gesture both casual and intimate. His nerves shivered. Not from fear of her touch, but from easy acceptance of her fingers on him. Which scared him to death. She was gorgeous and, probably like every other man in this room, he wanted to touch her and be touched by her. Their situation might be fake, but that didn't mean he wouldn't get the feelings.

"Relax. Not only do we seem to be compatible, but I have dated a guy or two. I know how to act."

He sniffed a laugh. "Sorry."

"It's okay. We're actually doing better than people on a real date because we're not afraid to be honest."

He fought a wince. She would not be pleased if he'd honestly tell her that her little ministrations with his bow tie had shot white-hot need through his veins. "I guess that's true."

"So if either one of us does anything wrong, we know we can be honest and tell the other one."

Okay. As long as they weren't admitting things like awakening hormones, he could get on board with that. "That's good."

She took his hand. "We are going to ace this."

He led the way to the table and introduced Eloise to his first business partner, Elias Greene, and his fiancée Bridget O'Malley, the couple getting married on Christmas Eve. As they sat down, another friend, George Russell and his wife, Andi, joined them.

When introduced, Eloise smiled and nodded, and the knots in Ricky's stomach began to unravel. He expected the husbands to fawn all over her, but he would have never guessed the wives would instantly like her.

Andi leaned over and caught Eloisa's hand. "I love your dress."

She laughed. "What? This old thing?"

Andi sniffed. "Okay. Don't tell me where you got it."

"Actually, I do a lot of my own designing."

Andi's mouth fell open. "You made that?"

"I bought it, then sort of reorganized it to suit my tastes."

Ricky liked the way she stuck with the truth. She didn't announce that she was broke, but she didn't pretend to be someone she wasn't. He took a sip from his water glass, his nerves settling and his faith in their deal reviving. She was doing very well.

They ate salad, filet mignon and simple baked potatoes, and an elaborate chocolate mousse creation for dessert, then Paul gave a toast that was more of a thank-you for coming and blessing to all in the new year, Then the dancing started.

Eloise turned to him with a smile. "I know you're dying to dance."

For the first time in his life, he wasn't. Her dress had no back. He was going to have to put his hands on *her.*

But his friends expected him to dance, so he gave her points for being a step ahead of the game.

He rose and took her hand. They threaded through the tables to the dance floor and kept going until they were in the center of the throng of people. This far into the dancers, they couldn't be seen by his friends at their table or even by anyone curious enough to seek them out.

As he pulled her to him, he let his hand fall to the small of her back and found soft, supple skin. But a quick mental review of her dress told him that if he were to lower his hands until he found fabric, he'd be fondling her butt.

Leaving his hand where it was, he cleared his throat. "Interesting back on this dress."

She laughed and winced. "Sorry."

"Oh, no. It's not a problem." *Most guys would kill for the opportunity to touch you like this.* But, of course, he didn't add that out loud. He looked down into her smiling face. "You seem like you're having fun."

"Honestly, the steak alone with worth the evening for me."

He twirled them around. "Not much steak in the diet of someone scrambling to make a living."

"Or champagne. Or even salad most days." She caught his gaze and smiled. "Thanks."

His heart flip-flopped. It had been a long time since he'd made someone happy. It humbled him that this woman was so broke she thanked him for food.

He winced. "You're welcome. But we still have to introduce you to a few people tonight, so you get your side of the arrangement too."

"Maybe tonight should just be my getting-my-feet-wet night." She glanced around. "Is this your usual crowd?"

"Usual crowd?"

"You know. Are these the people who typically get invited to the events you attend?"

Puzzled, he let his gaze ripple from face to face of the people on the dance floor. She was right. He did have a "usual" crowd. He'd see most of these people again and again until January second, when the party circuit would end.

"Yes. But other parties will have additional guests, depending on the event. You won't see any of these people at my office party. You'll see one or two at the fraternity reunion. You'll see them all at Elias and Bridget's wedding. And you probably saw most of them at Tucker and Olivia's."

He twirled them around again, and she laughed.

His gut tightened. Every instinct he had came to life. He couldn't remember the last time *he'd* made someone laugh. Or the last time he'd had fun. But he was having fun now.

When the music ended, he removed his hand from the softness that was the small of her back and immediately directed her to the couple beside them, Mimi and Oliver French.

She politely shook their hands. "I think I read about you in the *Journal* last week."

Oliver feigned humility. "I don't know why they wrote that piece."

Eloise laughed. "Because your firm made billions of dollars for your clients last year."

Mimi playfully swatted her husband's arm. "He's such a goose. Never likes to take credit. But we did have a banner year." She smiled at Eloise. "So tell me, dear, where did you get that dress?"

"A little boutique a few streets over from here," Eloise said with a smile. She didn't mention that it had been five years ago on a shopping trip with her mom. Or that the dress had been a conservative gown with a full back, high collar and slim belt to accent her waist. Andi might have loved hearing that, but Mimi behaved a little too much like Eloise's mom. She wouldn't see talent. She'd sniff out desperation.

"I must take a look at their stock."

"You really should."

"Eloise has only been in the city a short time," Ricky said, obviously having decided three years was a short time.

Oliver said, "Really."

"Yes." She smiled pleasantly. "I got my degree, and now I'm job hunting."

The band began to play. The couple smiled and turned away to dance again.

Ricky put his hand on the small of her back and they moved in time to the music.

"That went well."

"It did, but it feels odd." With the gooseflesh raised on her skin from his hand warming the small of her back, her voice came out a little huskier than she intended.

His eyebrows rose. "Feels odd?"

She carefully met his gaze. "Like I'm asking for a job."

He swung them around. "Okay. There's problem number one for you. You should be proud of the fact that you're looking for a job."

"I feel desperate."

"And that's problem number two. Do you think these people got to the top by not being able to smell desperation?"

"I know they can."

"You've gotta get rid of that."

"Okay."

The dance ended, and their conversation was cut short by someone else who came up to talk to Ricky. Unlike the Mr. and Mrs. French, this guy was not interested in Ricky's date. Not at all. Proposing a new business venture, he'd barely reacted when Ricky introduced her.

Eloise looked around. The winking diamonds shimmering through the crowd on throats, wrists and fingers told the story of just how rich, just how important, these people were. Yet Ricky looked totally comfortable. Listening as he explained that he couldn't invest because of the upcoming release of his new line of children's video games after which he would take that company public, she realized he was so casual because he was so smart. He belonged here. He was as sharp as any billionaire, any magnate, any tycoon.

Ridiculous pride surged in her. The whole group wanted to know his thoughts on something, but he was with *her*.

She shook her head to clear it of the unexpected thought. He wasn't with her because he liked her. He was with her because they'd made a deal, and he'd only made a deal because he needed protection. She was nothing more than a symbol to his friends that he had moved beyond the breakup that must have really hurt him.

She had best remember that.

After the set of waltzes, the band began to play a slow,

mellow tune. Expecting Ricky to bow out and direct her back to the table, she was surprised when he pulled her close.

She met the solid wall of his chest as his hand slid up her back, raising gooseflesh that she prayed he couldn't feel. Snuggled against him like a lover, she had to fight the urge to close her eyes and melt into him.

He's not a real date.

He's not a real date.

He's not a real date.

She rolled the litany through her brain until it sunk in. She'd had her Prince Charming and he was gone. If she didn't find a way to stop her reactions to Ricky, she might just lose the chance to continue going out with him.

Then there'd be no job. No future. Just endless days of temp jobs, struggling for rent money and eating packaged noodles.

CHAPTER THREE

REMINDING HERSELF OF her dire straits did not stem Eloise's attraction.

Dancing with Ricky and watching him between dances, it was obvious that he was strong and smart. And he treated her like royalty. He brought her drinks, eased her into most conversations and basically behaved as if she were someone he cared about…like a real date.

Was it any wonder she was having trouble separating fact from fiction?

The second time they slow danced, she'd felt a stirring inside her that went beyond attraction. She liked him. A lot. So she spent a little extra time in the ladies' room, reminding herself again this was only a deal, not a relationship.

But every time they slow danced, her reactions increased. Warmth flooded her when he held her. Pinpricks of delight raced through her when he did something sweet. He smiled at her when he held her cape for her at the end of the night, and her heart about shot out of her chest.

She groaned internally, finally figuring out what was wrong. Her brain might know this was only an act, but her body and her hormones reacted as if it were real.

Sliding into the limo, she sat as far away from him as she could.

As Norman started the engine, Ricky tapped his hands on his knees, studied her for a few seconds and finally said,

"Tomorrow night's event is a private dinner at the home of an investment banker who is also a college buddy."

From the far end of the seat, she smiled politely. "Sounds nice."

"I don't think you'll need to wear anything fancy."

"Probably not. A cocktail dress should be good."

"Great."

The conversation died, and Eloise leaned back. It was clear from his nervous gestures that he wasn't feeling any of the attraction she felt. So, if he'd noticed her over-long glances or the way she snuggled into him when they danced, that might be why he was so uncomfortable with her now.

She winced. Gazing into his eyes, nestling into him when they danced, she was breaking rule number one of their bargain: no romance. And if she didn't watch herself, he could end this deal.

To head off the curiosities of his driver, she politely let him walk her to her door—up all four flights of stairs, just in case the chauffer was the type to sneak into the building and check on things.

Outside her apartment, she smiled. "I had a great time." Too great. She'd been so angry with her parents and just plain life in general for so long that she'd never anticipated she'd actually enjoy going out again. Or that she'd be so attracted to someone again. And now here she was nervous, with their deal in jeopardy, trying not to look smitten.

He shoved his hands into his trouser pockets. "Thanks. I had a good time too."

She cleared her throat. "So. Um. Okay." Stammering. Great. Now she looked like an even bigger fool. Knowing how to end this torment, she caught the gaze of his dark, sleepy eyes and simply said, "Good night."

He stepped back. "Good night."

She turned, opened her door and jumped inside.

Braced against the solid steel, she groaned. What the

hell was she doing? She needed a job! Since when did she let a man tempt her like this?

They were in an arrangement. They were not dating. She could not lose this opportunity to make contacts that might net her a job just because her hormones had unexpectedly awakened. Particularly because *he* was not feeling anything for her.

And wouldn't that be humiliating? Her growing to like a guy who'd essentially hired her to be a date?

She'd had her fair share of mortification in her life, thank you very much. She wouldn't be so stupid again.

Ricky jogged down the stairs. Eloise had been the absolute perfect date. Gorgeous. A cuddler when they danced. She even had *him* believing she liked him. She was so perfect, he found himself humming as he jumped back into the limo.

But the second he realized he was humming, he thought of Blake and cursed. What right did he have to be happy when his son, his baby, was gone? He'd been as responsible for the death of his beautiful baby boy as Blake's mother had been. He did not deserve to be happy.

As Norman pulled the car out into the street, his phone rang. He automatically pulled it from his pocket and glanced at caller ID. His head research and development guy. He had to take it.

"What's up, Tom?"

"I'm sorry, Ricky. We hit a snag."

"A snag? We're in production. There shouldn't be any R&D snags."

"Which is why you might want to call your lawyer. A manufacturer in Berlin has just released a game exactly like game number two in your three-game package."

His stomach fell. "Are you kidding me?"

"No. I have a team comparing the games. Unfortunately,

it will take days. But that gives you time to call your lawyers and bring everybody into the loop."

"I want to know the very second you have a verdict."

He disconnected the call and dialed his lawyers.

At six the following evening, he hung up from yet another call with his R&D team. He hadn't slept, hadn't eaten. He felt like his phone was growing out of his ear. Exhausted, he considered not going to Tim and Jennifer's dinner party. But, in the end, he knew missing the quiet gathering of friends might spur more questions than he cared to deal with. Until he figured out whether he and a German manufacturer had come up with the same game at the same time, or one of his employees had sold his idea, he had to pretend nothing was wrong. And, luckily, he already had Eloise Vaughn in place.

He knocked on her door. She opened it with a smile and immediately handed him her black wool cape.

Sliding it on her shoulders, he said, "You look great."

She did. Even in a simple black dress and pearls, she was a knockout. His eyes might be heavy from lack of sleep, and his brain dead from conversations about patents and corporate spies, but he still could see she was gorgeous.

She turned and smiled at him. "You look great, too."

He glanced down at his black suit with a white shirt and thin black tie. "Think I'm okay for a dinner party?"

"You have squarely hit semiformal. You'll be fine."

She headed for the door and all but ran down the four flights of stairs to the building lobby. Tired, he could barely keep up with her. He wondered again about the wisdom of not canceling this party. He hadn't had any sleep, and her running was odd, as if she were trying to get this night over with. That wouldn't be good at all for their charade. She raced outside to the limo and, after Norman opened the door for her, slid in.

Two steps behind her, Ricky got in beside her. "You're in a hurry tonight."

"I'm just nervous."

"Don't be. Tim and Jennifer are very casual." He stifled a yawn.

Relief swooshed through her. Not just because he'd eased her fears about the dinner party, but because he'd almost yawned. He wasn't nervous around her anymore. If anything, he seemed bored, which had to mean she was successfully hiding her attraction to him. As long as she played it cool, the deal would not be in jeopardy.

She straightened on the seat and smiled at him. "I'll be fine."

Ricky's cell phone rang and he sighed. "I have to take this."

She waved her hand in dismissal, grateful for any chance to look like a woman who wasn't interested in him. "No problem." She smiled. "Take the call."

He clicked the button to answer his phone, and she glanced out the window at the city, which was beginning to dress up for the holiday. Tall Christmas trees had been erected in the lobbies of office buildings, their lights twinkling in the darkness. Shop windows featured elaborate Christmas displays. Salvation Army bell ringers stood beside street vendors with carts covered in tinsel. Steam rose from manhole covers.

Ricky was still on the phone when the driver pulled up to a luxury apartment building and opened the door. He talked as he got out of the limo, talked as they walked to the door and finally disconnected the call when the doorman offered them entry.

"Sorry about that."

Fake date smile in place, Eloise happily said, "It's fine. Really. You don't need to apologize." She gave him a significant look. "Remember?"

He frowned. "Right."

Drat! Now she'd gone too far in the other direction. Instead of reassuring him, she was behaving like a hired hand. Exactly what he didn't want.

They rode up in the elevator in silence. The doors opened onto a plush penthouse. A huge Christmas tree stood in front of a wall of windows. Bright lights and tinsel had been strung around the tree, and that theme continued on coffee tables and archways. Two red stockings decorated the marble fireplace mantel. Awash in lights and color, the main room had a warm, cozy, old-fashioned Christmas feel.

Tim and Jennifer welcomed them with hugs, got them drinks and slid them into the group of couples in front of the elegantly simple marble fireplace.

Conversation flowed easily until the butler announced dinner was served. The hostess pointed out seats at the long mahogany table set with fine china and crystal. Once everyone was comfortable and salads had been served, the lively discussion resumed.

Something light and airy floated through Eloise. Amid the colorful Christmas lights, tinsel and easygoing people, she totally relaxed. This was her second meal, good wine and simple conversation in two days, but, best of all, the odd tension between herself and her fake date had evaporated. With no dancing or touching of any kind required, she didn't have to worry about her attraction or his lack of attraction. All she had to do was talk. And that came easily.

After dinner, the men retreated to the den for a cigar.

Proud of herself for controlling her attraction to Ricky, Eloise breathed a sigh of relief. But when she turned to the women seated with her in front of the fireplace, she found herself facing four round-eyed wives.

"I thought he'd never date again."

Glad for the chance to really play her role and fulfill her commitment, she smiled as she picked up her wineglass. "Oh, he wasn't such a tough nut to crack."

Jennifer's face fell. "Sweetie, it was four months after the tragedy before he even *spoke* to anyone."

Eloise kept her facial features neutral, but internally she winced. Wasn't *tragedy* a bit of an odd way to refer to a breakup?

Muriel, who owned a string of restaurants and was married to Fred, who Eloise had learned was the prankster of their fraternity, said, "Fred was positive he was going to lose everything. All his businesses and all his prospects for more business. But then..." She turned to Jennifer. "What was it? Six months in, he finally picked himself up and got back to work."

And wasn't missing six months of work a bit extreme for a breakup?

Surely she'd misinterpreted.

"He missed work for six months?"

"Oh, sweetie, I don't think he ate for six months."

Her heart stuttered. This had been no ordinary breakup. Everything inside her wanted to ask what had happened. But she caught herself before she opened her mouth. She was supposed to be dating Ricky. These women assumed she knew—assumed *he'd told her*—about whatever had happened. If she didn't behave accordingly, she'd ruin everything.

She quietly said, "It was a difficult time for him."

Jennifer patted her hand. "Which is why we are so glad he found someone."

She smiled. "I'm glad he found me, too." She replied easily enough, but her brain began to scramble for answers. What kind of breakup hit a man so hard he didn't work for six months?

She told herself to stop. Told herself that if he wanted her to know, he'd tell her. She even told herself that she might not want to know because knowing might draw them closer, and she was already having trouble separating fact from fiction.

But nothing worked. Curiosity tightened her chest, filled her brain, wouldn't let her think of anything else.

Forty minutes later, the men ambled out of the den. Everyone had work the next morning. Apparently Ricky had a conference call with lawyers in Berlin, so he had to be up the earliest, which made them the first out the door.

He slid her black wool cape over her shoulders and directed her into the elevator.

Though part of her knew it was overstepping the boundaries of their deal, her curiosity and her genuine concern for him were too much to handle. As soon as she and Ricky were alone in the elevator, she intended to ask him what had happened.

But two seconds before the door closed, Dennis Margolis and his wife, Binnie, jumped in with them.

Dennis rubbed his hands together. "It's gonna feel even colder out there after sitting by that fire."

Binnie sighed dreamily. "I don't care. I hope it stays cold. We need snow for Christmas. The season is so much more fun when there's a coating of snow on the decorations. Don't you think, Eloise?"

"Um, yeah. I love snow. Especially for the holiday."

She smiled at Ricky, expecting him to smile back. He did, but it was a weak lift of his lips. Either he was really tired or "man time" in the den had not gone well.

As they walked through the lobby and into the frigid air and the limo, his phone rang again. She climbed into the car, but he shut the door and stood on the sidewalk talking. Twenty minutes later, Norman opened the door again. He slid in with a big smile.

"Good news?"

"More like major disaster averted. I thought I was going to have to go to war with a company in Europe, but turns out somebody just made a mistake. Once our R&D people went over the games in question with a fine-tooth comb, they realized we'd panicked prematurely."

She had no idea what he was talking about, but his company, his business, wasn't really her concern right now. "That's great."

"It's excellent. I expect a problem or two before every rollout, but it's nice when they resolve themselves so easily."

Glad he was in a better mood, she nonetheless waited a few minutes, until they were solidly in traffic, before she said, "Your friends' wives are really happy to see you dating."

"Um-hum."

Nerves filled her. How the hell did someone say, "So, what's the tragedy in your life?"

She licked her lips, gathering her courage. She couldn't handle the curiosity. But more than that, if his friends discovered she didn't know, it might ruin their charade. "They assume I know what happened to you."

He turned to her, his previously sleepy brown eyes suddenly cool and distant. "I'm sure they do."

She swallowed. Caught in the gaze she didn't recognize, dark, scary eyes of a stranger, she faltered. "So maybe you should tell me?"

He glanced out the window, then back at her. "One of the reasons I'm comfortable with you is that you don't know."

She frowned. "But wouldn't the charade make more sense if I knew?"

"Not if you pity me."

Pity him? What the hell had happened to him? "How about if I promise not to pity you?"

"You can't make that promise."

She glanced out the window. "What if somebody tells me? I mean, what if we get separated again and somebody just blurts it out?"

"I guess you and I will just have to stay close so that no one does."

She snapped her gaze to his. A combination of fear

and curiosity rumbled up from her chest. She was already fighting an attraction to this guy. Did she really want to be close to him? Every time they were out? Spend every minute together?

How had such a simple plan become so complicated?

After walking Eloise to her door, Ricky ran down the four flights of stairs and ambled to his limo. Once he was inside, Norman started the engine and headed out.

He'd been having a great time at the party, so great he'd actually enjoyed the ribbing he took from his friends about Eloise being too beautiful for a guy like him.

Then they'd gotten into the limo and she'd asked about Blake, and he felt as if he'd been hit by a train. He hadn't thought about his son in two days. He'd been so preoccupied with his work problems and pretend-dating that he'd forgotten his son. *His baby. His whole world for eighteen months.*

How could he forget him?

He tapped on the glass between himself and Norman. It slid open.

"Take me to the hospital."

Norman caught his gaze in the rearview mirror. "It's midnight."

"I have my key card and identification."

The glass closed. Ricky sat back, letting the air slowly leach out of his lungs. The pain that had been his constant companion reclaimed him. Thirty minutes later, the limo stopped. His door opened and he climbed out.

He used his card to get into the hospital. Even, determined steps took him through the silent lobby and up to the Intensive Care Unit for the children's ward.

He stopped in front of the wall of glass, staring at the sweet, innocent children struggling for life.

"Mr. Langley?"

He faced Regina Grant, night shift supervisor. "Good evening, Regina."

"Everything okay?"

"Everything's fine." But she knew why he was here. When they rededicated the wing, after his generous donation had renovated the floor and bought new equipment, she'd been the one who'd seen his distress. She'd cornered him in a room, and rather than extol him with platitudes, she'd told him to count his blessings. "If you can't think of any blessings...come here. Look through that window. Realize you do not have it as bad as some."

The memory made him shake his head. He missed his son. He missed him with a longing that lodged in his throat, tormented his soul. He wished he'd done a million things differently. And he hated that a work problem and a pretty girl had made him forget his little boy.

But so many people did have it so much worse.

"I'm just here reminding myself I don't have it as bad as some."

"You really don't. And life does go on."

Sadness rippled through him. Memories of his son's giggle, the warmth of his child's hug, that simple trust floated back. But along with it came an odd, unfamiliar fear. Life might go on, but he didn't want to forget his son. Never. Ever.

After a prolonged silence, Regina caught his forearm. "Here's a thought. Instead of visiting in the middle of the night, maybe what you need is a little interaction."

He faced her. "With the kids?"

"Yes."

"They're too sick." And he was too afraid.

"These are. But if you'd come at regular visiting hours and go to the left instead of the right when you get off the elevator, I'm sure the nurses could set it up so that you could read to the kids in their playroom."

He said nothing. She turned to go but stopped and faced

him again. "Cheering up some kids who need cheering would be better than staring at kids you can't help."

Sucking in his breath, he watched her go, wondering what the hell was wrong with him. He'd been preoccupied with business before and as soon as the crisis was over, memories of Blake had come in an avalanche. The difference this time was Eloise.

He couldn't let his fake date make him forget his son. Or his guilt. And if she did, he had to stop this.

CHAPTER FOUR

MONDAY MORNING ELOISE awoke to the real world. She dressed in work trousers and a thick sweater, then bundled herself in her quilted parka, a scarf and mittens. She rode the subway to Manhattan and an ordinary, crowded elevator to the twenty-ninth-floor law offices of Pearson, Pearson, Leventry and Downing.

She slipped off her mittens and scarf and hung her coat on the coat tree in the corner of the tiny space she shared with ten filing cabinets and the desk of Tina Horner.

Tina entered rubbing her hands together. "It should snow. Then even though it would still be cold, we'd at least have festive snow to make it feel Christmas-y."

"I was just talking about that with someone last night."

"So I'm not the only one who thinks we're being cheated by cold weather without snow."

Eloise sat at her desk, then hit the button to boot up her computer. "Nope, Binnie Margolis is right with you."

"Binnie Margolis?" Tina whistled. "Somebody's moved up in the world."

Eloise laughed. "Not hardly. I'm doing a favor for a friend, going to a few Christmas parties with him so he doesn't get hounded because he doesn't have a date."

Tina shrugged out of her coat. "So it's like going out with your cousin?"

Eloise winced. She absolutely did not have cousin-like feelings for Ricky Langley. But she wouldn't tell Tina that.

"Not exactly. But in exchange for me going out with him, he agreed to introduce me around in the hope that I'd make a connection and maybe find a real job."

Tina took her seat at the desk across from Eloise. "That sounds promising."

"It is. Or it would be—"

"Except?"

She bit her lower lip, wondering if she should come clean with Tina. She decided she needed to talk to someone. "Except I'm thinking I should end our deal."

"End a deal that might help you find a job? Are you nuts?"

"More like concerned. I thought he wanted a date because of a bad breakup, but the way the wives of his friends were talking last night I get the feeling something big happened to this guy."

"Big like what?"

"Something tragic. They said, 'after his tragedy' a couple of times."

Tina winced. "Sounds like maybe his last girlfriend died."

Oh. Wouldn't that make sense? "Could be."

"Too bad we're not allowed to use the internet here or we could look him up."

"I can always go to the library after work."

"Maybe you should."

Knowing she could investigate him later, she relaxed and got down to the business of typing legal briefs. Because she worked late that night, she couldn't go to the library. Disappointment and curiosity collided, making her too nervous to sleep.

As she lay in bed pondering Ricky, their deal and her life, it dawned on her that since she'd met him, she'd been immersed in helping him. All weekend long, she'd remade dresses, gone to parties and worked to make a good impression on his friends so he could be happy. And it had felt good. Really good. She'd been busy. Happy. Until his friends' wives talked about "his tragedy" she'd been enjoying this charade.

And thinking of someone else had made her stop dwelling on her own problems. She hadn't done that since her husband had died.

Maybe she shouldn't jeopardize their good rapport by looking him up.

Maybe helping a man with a tragedy in his past was exactly what she needed to get over her own grief.

Especially because he was a friend of a friend. Ricky Langley wouldn't be in Tucker Engle's circle of confidantes if there was something wrong with him.

He was a guy with a tragic past. A guy she could help. And in return she could forget about her own troubles.

Ricky trudged up Eloise's four flights of steps on Friday night, so sad he'd nearly canceled their evening together again. On Monday night, he'd gone to the hospital to read to the kids, as Regina had suggested, and it had been devastating. He hated seeing kids suffer. He couldn't believe Regina had suggested he read to children so weak they broke his heart, reminded him of Blake, reminded him of how stupid he'd been. His son was dead because he'd never asked Blake's mother to let him raise him. She was a party girl turned mother and he'd seen the difficulties she'd had fitting Blake into her life. She probably would have been happy to give him custody of Blake, as long as she got visitation, but he'd never asked.

Anger with himself had made his pulse race, and that night, he couldn't stay in the children's ward activity room. He'd bowed out before the kids even knew he'd come there to read, so there was no harm done to them. But as he'd struggled to get through his week without thinking of

Blake, without berating himself for not asking for custody, for not taking his son away from a woman who clearly wanted an out, he'd simply forgotten about Eloise Vaughn.

He almost laughed. Another man would think it impossible that he could forget a woman so beautiful she could be a princess. But that was his life.

When she opened her door to him, and he looked down at her dress, he blinked. The pale blue fabric complemented her pink skin tone and yellow hair, but it also glittered as if someone had woven tinsel into the material. She looked like a princess trapped in a snow globe.

His heart lifted a bit. "Wow."

She smiled. "You know, even if nothing else comes of fake dating you, I'm getting a real sense of satisfaction out of your compliments on my sewing."

He took her cape. When she turned for him to help her into it, he noticed this dress had a full back and sighed with relief. The gloom that hung over him like a dome loosened a bit. "You deserve to be complimented. I'd never guess you were taking old clothes and making them new."

They headed down the hall to the stairs. "It's not like I'm redoing things from the last century. Five years ago, my clothes were in style."

"Then you went to university and your money had to go for tuition."

She stopped at the top step and faced him. "Something like that."

"Hey, unless you're born into money, you're going to suffer through university."

A strange expression crossed her face. He wouldn't be this far in his business dealings if he couldn't read the look of someone who had something to say. The pinch of pain in her eyes told him it wasn't something good.

But instead of a confession, she said, "Or starve."

He smiled, but curiosity ruffled through him. She'd told him about her job problem, but it had never crossed his mind to think she might have had personal troubles in her past. Something that had broken her heart.

Still, he pushed it from his mind. He had problems of his own. And wondering about her wasn't part of their deal. Getting to know her wasn't even part of their deal. In fact, with as pretty as she was and as tempting, he might be wise not to ask questions.

In the limo, they talked generically about her job and his busy schedule as they drove to a hotel in the theater district. Lit for Christmas, Times Square took his breath away. So many lights. So much creativity in the Santa and sleigh that rode the tickertape around the jumbo video screens, and the Santa's workshop filled with elves in the toy store windows.

He shoved back the memory of bringing Blake here for a private tour of the toy store and focused on getting himself and Eloise out of the limo.

Again, the night was cold and, as they stepped out, Eloise shivered. His arm rose in a natural reaction to pull her close, but just before he would have touched her, he stopped himself.

Too many things happened naturally with this woman, and although that probably added to the success of their charade, it wasn't good for either of them personally. When they weren't actually at a party, he would keep his distance.

A small stairway took them to the hotel lobby, where they were directed to an elevator to the ballroom. Lively music blared at them as the doors opened.

Eloise turned to him. "Are we late?"

"No. We're right on time. Preston's a music promoter. Expect the unexpected. Including the fact that he might have started the party early just because he wanted to."

"Cool."

A laugh escaped, and he relaxed a little. Technically, he had to have fun and talk to her for the charade to work. "Cool? Maybe yes. Maybe no. But I'm betting on no."

She happily exited the elevator and nearly walked into

Preston Jenkins's arms. High as a kite, their host took their coats and handed them off to a huge, beefy man who looked like a bodyguard.

He hugged Eloise effusively. "You are as gorgeous as the gossip mills are reporting."

Her eyes grew round and shiny with what looked to be fear, and Ricky remembered how she hadn't liked getting her picture taken the week before. Now she appeared deathly afraid of gossip.

"Which is why," Preston slurred, "I'm thrilled that we are about ten feet away from mistletoe."

Her eyes grew even larger, and this time Ricky understood. No woman wanted to be slobbered over by a stranger, regardless of how much mistletoe hung over doorways. Protectiveness rose up in him. She was *his* date. She wouldn't be here if he hadn't brought her. He needed to get her out of this.

His brain scrambled for a way to save her, and eventually he simply opened his mouth and said, "Do you really think I'd let a schmoozer like you kiss my date?"

Preston slapped his arm. "Oh, such a kidder. I wasn't going to kiss her. I'm getting pictures of everybody kissing their *dates* under the mistletoe." He pointed to the huge bodyguard type, who displayed a camera.

His heart did something that felt like a samba. "You want me to kiss Eloise?"

Nudging Eloise and Ricky under the mistletoe, Preston grinned drunkenly. "Yeah. You kiss Eloise."

Happiness tumbled through him before he could stop it, before he could think of Blake, before he could think of the myriad reasons this was wrong. It was as if time froze and there was only him and Eloise and mistletoe. No crowd. No past. No future. Just a kiss.

Eloise blinked up at him. Her pretty blue eyes round and curious. The curls of her soft blond hair framing her face. Her pink lips parted.

His pulse scrambled. He hadn't kissed a woman in al-most two years. And just touching the skin of Eloise's back had set his hormones dancing. What would happen when their lips met?

Fireworks probably.

His pulse kicked up again. He hadn't felt fireworks in forever.

Longing, swift and sharp, rose up in him.

He silenced it. They were only fake dating. Kissing took them to dangerous ground.

Except he hadn't kissed a woman in almost two years. Hadn't felt alive in almost two years—

He glanced back at Preston, who waved dramatically. "Go on! Camera's waiting!"

He caught Eloise's gaze again. Need prickled his skin. Desire swelled. And he had to admit he wanted this. He wanted to feel alive again, if only for a few seconds. It was foolish. But it was also only a kiss. One kiss when he'd been so long deprived hardly seemed earth-shattering, and he could go back to being miserable after that. Plus, if he didn't kiss her, he would ruin their charade.

He bent his head and barely touched his mouth to hers. Soft, smooth lips met his. She tasted like peppermint and felt like heaven, and his head spun. Had he said this wouldn't be earth-shattering? He'd been wrong.

His mouth pressed against hers, and simple need bub-bled like a witch's brew in his gut. He knew he was flirt-ing with disaster. But he couldn't stop himself. He'd never wanted anything as much as he wanted to simply lose him-self in her. The softness, the sweetness he'd never found in another woman.

One kiss. Then he would walk away.

When Ricky's mouth shifted and he began to take, all the blood drained from Eloise's body, then returned in a grand whoosh of warm tingles. He'd touched his mouth to hers softly at first, in a kiss that felt almost experimental. Then his hands slid up her arms to her shoulders, and he pulled her just a little bit closer, pressed his lips a little bit harder and she melted.

She couldn't think. She couldn't breathe. Too many sensations bombarded her. The crisp scent of his aftershave. The power in the hands holding her shoulders. The softness of his mouth that pressed one second, then hesitated the next. He seemed to want this and fear it, and though she knew it was wrong, she opened her mouth and egged him on.

His hands tightened on her shoulders. Need crashed against need. The kiss deepened so fast, her knees might have buckled, but she wasn't paying any attention. She longed for the feeling of his tongue gliding along her tongue, his chest pressed against hers, his hands holding her shoulders.

He released her, and for two seconds they stared into each other's eyes. Then the music blaring from the ballroom registered, along with the sound of Preston laughing.

Standing by his bodyguard and studying the photo in the digital camera he said, "It's a great pic. You look fantastic. Young lovers. I adore you. Now move along."

Ricky gave a fake laugh and said something inane to Preston before he guided her into the ballroom. Her dress swooshed against her legs silkily and the scents of pine and vanilla permeating the room seemed strong and vibrant, as if kissing her fake date had brought all of her senses to life.

"Sorry about that."

"It's fine." She cleared her throat when her voice came out as a squeak. "Part of the deal."

But it wasn't fine. They'd taken that kiss too far, and it had been a mistake. She liked this guy. He was a good person with something sad enough in his past that his friends' wives called it a tragedy. They should keep their distance. Instead, they'd kissed and it had been amazing. Which was wrong. W...R...O...N...G. Because he didn't like her and she was going to get hurt.

They spent an uncomfortable half hour trying to make conversation as Ricky's friends, the people who would join them at their table, arrived. Her nerves continued as they ate dinner, danced and left the ballroom early, Ricky explaining to Preston that he had to rise before dawn for conference calls Sunday morning.

But in the limo on the way home, watching him sitting beside her, staring out the window, looking like a man lost, Eloise chastised herself. All night long, she'd held herself aloof, flummoxed by that kiss. This was a seriously unhappy guy and all he wanted was one nice Christmas, yet she couldn't stop thinking about herself. Her reactions to him. Her stupid hormones.

But that kiss had been one of the best of her life. If not *the* best. It was hard to stay objective after that.

She shook her head. What was she doing? She'd finally found a way to put some meaning in her life. She couldn't let one kiss distract her. Her back stiffened as she straightened on the limo seat. As God was her witness, she intended to give him what he really wanted. Christmas. A joyful, happy Christmas. No easing back into "the season," as he'd said the night they made their deal. No fake date. She would be someone who really cared about him and who gave him joy.

Ricky walked her to her apartment door and for a crazy second he thought about kissing her good-night. He couldn't get the mistletoe kiss out of his head. Or the expression of surprise on Eloise's face. He wanted to kiss her just to see it again.

What was he doing? He was too depressed, too wounded to bring a woman into his life.

At her door, she smiled politely. "The party was fun."

He sniffed in derision. "Preston's a freak."

"Or a guy who likes to have a good time." She straightened his bow tie, smoothed her hands down his top coat collar. "Maybe we should work a little harder to have some fun?"

He studied her face, her pretty blue eyes, warm pink mouth and sweet smile. She was serious. She wanted him to have fun.

Syrupy warmth flooded his blood. A strange feeling tightened his chest, and although it took him a few seconds, he realized it was affection.

He wasn't just attracted to her. He was beginning to like her.

But he knew that was wrong.

He stepped back. "Or maybe we should just put in an appearance at these things and leave early all the time?"

He turned and started down the stairs without waiting for Eloise to answer. No matter what happened at the rest of the parties, he wouldn't kiss her again.

The next morning, he called to tell Eloise she only needed to wear jeans and a sweater to that night's party, his fraternity reunion. The lilt of her voice tiptoed though him, reminding him of the kiss the day before, and he hung up as quickly as he could and lost himself in work.

That was the best way to deal with feelings—remorse over Blake, unwanted curiosity about Eloise. Work was the way to forget and give himself some peace.

When his phone rang a few hours later, he answered absently. "Yes?"

Tucker Engle laughed. "Is that any way to greet a friend?"

Tossing his pen to his desk, Ricky leaned back. "No." He laughed. "Sorry. How's Kentucky?"

"We're knee-deep in sledding and hot cocoa."

Ricky smirked. It was hard to imagine workaholic Tucker spending five or six weeks in the country. "Bored?"

"No. Actually, I'm enjoying it so much that I don't want to leave, but I've had an emergency crop up and I need your help."

Ricky sat up. After everything Tucker had done for him, he'd love a chance to do a favor in return. "What can I do?"

"I need to put in an appearance at a meeting for one of the companies I'm heavily invested in. I just need a presence. Somebody who can give my opinion."

"I'll be happy to go. Tell me the address and the date."

"It's today. I know it's Saturday, so if you can't go, it's okay."

"No. I'm happy to do it."

Tucker covered the details with Ricky, who made a few notes, but only a few, because there wasn't much for Ricky to do except make one brief statement.

Still, Tucker's reply showed he was grateful. "Thanks again."

"You're welcome. It's not a big deal. If it runs long, I'll just call Eloise and tell her we'll be late for my frat reunion."

Even as he said it, Ricky realized his mistake.

Tucker pounced. "So, you and Eloise hit it off on that ride home after the party?"

He winced. "You could say that."

"Good. You've been down too long, and Eloise could use a little pick-me-up, too. She's had some rough patches."

Ricky's eyes narrowed. Pretty, sweet Eloise had had some rough patches? Just from the tone of Tucker's voice, he could tell this was about more than her inability to get a job. He remembered the expression that flitted over her face when they'd talked about college. Obviously Tucker knew something Ricky didn't.

He opened his mouth to ask but couldn't. It didn't seem right or fair to ask questions about a woman who was only attending a few parties with him.

He wasn't supposed to care.

He *didn't* care.

He didn't need to know.

But even an hour after Ricky hung up the phone, as he dressed to go to Tucker's meeting, he couldn't get that odd look in Eloise's eyes out of his head. Curiosity overwhelmed him, so he typed her name into his computer's search engine.

Late Saturday afternoon, Eloise began getting dressed. That evening's party was Ricky's informal fraternity reunion, held in a pub in midtown. When he'd called that morning, he'd told her to just wear jeans and a sweater.

Still, knowing how men were about pride in front of fraternity brothers, and back to her mission of making sure he had a good time, Eloise dressed with care. She slid into an emerald green cashmere sweater that she'd been saving for a special occasion, fixed her hair in a long ponytail and applied just the right amount of makeup to look cheerful and festive.

She would get this guy out of his misery if it killed her.

He arrived, helped her into her parka and led her down the stairs.

"This might be like hell week."

She laughed. The fact that he hadn't mentioned putting in an appearance and leaving early encouraged her. "You think I can't handle a roomful of men and their dates?"

He paused at the door and looked back at her. "Some won't have dates."

"Oh."

He started walking again, and she stood rooted to her spot. He had to be in his midthirties. The people he went to school with would be about the same age, but they wouldn't have dates?

What did that mean?

When he reached the limo, Norman opened the door. Realizing she was standing in the lobby like a ninny, she scrambled to catch up. As soon as they were settled, Norman took off.

"So you're married."

Surprise kicked the air out of her lungs and made her forget all about the fact that some of his fraternity buddies wouldn't have dates. "What?"

He faced her, his eyes cool and direct. "You're married. I found your marriage license through a quick internet search and didn't find a divorce decree. Ergo, you're married."

Her heart galloped. Her nerve endings jumped. Every ounce of blood fell to her feet as every possible answer she could give him winged through her brain. But none of them would work. Shock and anger collided to create a horrible sourness in the pit of her stomach.

"For a guy who has his fair share of secrets, you're certainly not shy about uncovering mine."

"Believe it or not, I searched your name because I felt bad for you. I could tell from how you avoided the topic of college that something had happened and I wanted to know what."

His voice was soft, honest, but tinged with a bit of hurt. And why not? He thought he was going out with a married woman.

She sucked in a breath and said the words that didn't just pinch her heart; they filled her with shame. "My husband died."

The expression of concern that came over his face was totally unexpected. "Your husband died?"

She nodded.

He sighed in obvious disgust with himself. "I'm sorry. I was just so flabbergasted to find the marriage license and no divorce degree that I didn't look any further." He shook his head. "You're so young. I never in a million years thought to look for a death certificate." He shook his head again. "I am so sorry."

"If it made you so angry to find the marriage license

and no divorce decree, why didn't you just call and cancel?" But before he could answer, she figured it out on her own, and she gasped. "You hoped I had an explanation."

"I need you. I need this charade. Plus, you've been nothing but a nice person around me." He shrugged. "It was only fair that I give you a chance to explain."

Hope filled the black hole of shame that lived where her heart should have been. Laura Beth and Olivia accepted her, understood her. But she'd never had the courage to test another person's feelings about her. She wasn't supposed to care if Ricky Langley liked her. But it was suddenly, incomprehensibly important that he hear the story and understand.

"I fell for a guy with tattoos and a motorcycle and ran off with him. Although we loved each other, getting married was a huge mistake. It took only two months before I realized we were in trouble. He sat at home or in his buddy's garage, talking bikes and drinking beer all day."

His eyes sought hers, but he said nothing.

Shame and fear shivered through her, but she trudged on.

"I spent every day supporting him by waitressing." She glanced down at her hands, then back up at him. "This story makes me sound like I quit loving him when he refused to support me, but the truth was I never stopped loving him. I just knew we'd made a mistake getting married. I was about to leave him—"

"When he was killed on his bike and you were free."

A shard of pain sliced through her. For a guy who clearly hoped she'd redeem herself, he certainly was quick to find the dark cloud. "When he was diagnosed with cancer. I spent three months taking him to doctor's appointments, helping him through chemo, cleaning up messes, offering words of hope. That's when we started talking. It killed him that he couldn't find work, so he masked his pain by pretending not to care that I had to support him. I reacted by getting angrier and angrier with a guy who was already hurting, filled with shame." She stopped and closed her eyes. "Then he died, and I've spent the past years angry with myself." She opened her eyes. "Feeling guilty. Feeling desperately wrong. I hadn't left him, but I was about to and he would have died alone."

He studied her silently, then finally said, "I'm sorry."

This time she looked away. "It certainly wasn't your fault."

"No. But I shouldn't have probed into your private life."

The limo stopped. Norman opened the door and they stepped out.

Memories followed her up the sidewalk and beneath the portico, tormenting her with the knowledge that she'd been immature and foolish. Not in marrying Wayne, but in almost leaving. True, she'd stayed and nursed him until he'd died. But if he'd visited the doctor one week later, she would have been gone. The man she'd loved would have died alone.

When they walked into the pub, the noise of the crowd swelled over her, along with the scents of corned beef and cabbage. Ricky directed her to the room in the back, where round tables were partially filled with men his age. The pool table entertained six or eight tall, lean guys and two dartboards had the attention of another four or five.

Only about seven women, dates of the guys laughing and talking, were there. More than twenty guys but only seven women. And three of them she recognized—Jennifer, Muriel and Binnie. In spite of the trauma over telling her story, Eloise almost smiled. Ricky must have been in the geek fraternity.

"Hey, it's Ricky."

Everybody faced them. He shrugged out of his leather jacket and hung it on a hook on the wall before he turned and took her coat. She swallowed. Nice shoulders and a solid chest filled his warm amber sweater to perfection. His jeans all but caressed his perfect butt.

Before she could chastise herself for noticing, his mouth fell open slightly as his gaze rippled down her emerald green sweater to her tight jeans and tall black boots.

With her story out and his fear that she was a liar alleviated, she smiled in question. He'd brought her to the party to continue the charade for his own benefit, but he knew her now. And the confidence she could muster as a fake date suddenly seemed all wrong. Now, she was herself. Eloise Cummings Vaughn—not just struggling working girl, but also widow. She needed a word, something from him, that let her know things between them were okay.

He leaned in. "You look fantastic. But you always look fantastic. Thank you for doing this for me."

His warm breath tickled her ear. He smelled great. And his words told her what she needed to hear. They were back in good standing. She might be a real person to him now, but she was still a fake date.

A tall, thin guy wearing a sweater with a Santa face plastered across the front strolled over. Handing Ricky a pool cue, he said, "You beat me four games straight last year. This year I intend to win."

Ricky took the stick but glanced at Eloise.

This wasn't her party. It was his. Plus, telling him about her past hadn't changed her mission. If anything, it had strengthened it. She'd stayed too long in her self-pity. She'd lingered too long with her guilt. If the best way to get out was to help someone else, she would help him.

She smiled. "Hey, go. Enjoy yourself. I'll be fine."

She turned to walk over to the women, who had all gathered in a cluster but, on second thought, faced him. "Can I get you a beer?"

He smiled. Really smiled.

Their gazes caught and held, as one door of their relationship closed and another squeaked open. She was no longer a poor girl who needed his help. She was a woman who'd confided her past. He wasn't just a rich guy who wanted a date. He'd listened. He hadn't judged. He'd sympathized.

"Yeah. Thanks."

"Pitchers are all on a table in the back," the guy who'd challenged Ricky to the pool game said. "Help yourself pizza and wings, too. We don't stand on ceremony. It's self-serve."

She smiled at Ricky again. "I'll be right back."

She got him a beer and put two pieces of pizza on a paper plate for him. She took them to a table near the pool game, pointed them out for Ricky and walked over to the gaggle of women.

"All right. Spill. Who are you, and how the hell did you get Ricky to go out, especially at Christmas?"

Holding the glass of beer she'd poured for herself, she smiled at the dates of his fraternity brothers. "As I told Binnie, Muriel and Jennifer on Sunday, we met at the Christmas party of a mutual friend."

"Tucker Engle," a short, dark-haired woman supplied. "Jeremy and I were there and we saw you. That means you haven't known each other long." She stuck out her hand to shake Eloise's. "I'm Misty, by the way. I date the tall guy over there." She pointed at a true geek with glasses and a sweater vest. "Jeremy."

"Nice to meet you."

The remaining women introduced themselves, but as the conversation moved on, thoughts of Sunday's dinner party came back to her. Especially Muriel and Jennifer talking about his tragedy.

She glanced back at Ricky. When she'd told him about Wayne, she'd handed him the perfect opportunity to tell her his trauma and he hadn't taken it.

She tried to tell herself it didn't matter, that their relationship was only an arrangement, but tonight that argument didn't float. Not because she liked him or because the new feelings that had sprung up made the situation feel real. It was because she suddenly realized she might be fulfilling her end of their bargain, but he wasn't doing anything about his. He hadn't gotten her one interview. Not one.

She was doing everything he wanted, even confiding her secrets, but he wasn't doing anything for her.

It wasn't long before everyone had congregated together at a table. Soon, they pulled a second table over and then a third. As Ricky played game after game of pool, he watched Eloise kick back and chat, sip beer and eat a piece of pizza.

He was glad. He didn't know how his search had missed the death certificate of her husband, except that he hadn't been looking for a death certificate but a divorce decree. When he hadn't found one, he'd gotten angry and stopped searching.

He'd tried to rationalize her situation with the fact that every time he'd gone to her apartment, he'd only seen signs of two women living there. No man. No husband. And his internet search had confirmed that she worked as a temp in New York City, but she'd married in Kentucky. He'd assumed she'd left the bad marriage behind and was waiting until she could afford a divorce. Which wasn't a crime, but it was something she should have told him.

So her story in the limo had stopped him short. Especially the part about the guilt. Lord knows he understood guilt over someone dying. Most people understood the grief. He understood the guilt.

He started another game, but noticed that his fraternity brothers were ambling toward the tables with the women. They pulled chairs behind the chairs of their dates, but those without dates—and there were plenty—seemed to be congregating around Eloise.

As he played pool with Jonathan Hopewell, the laughter

from the now crowded tables rolled over to him. He glanced up and saw Kyle Banister, who was seated on a chair behind Eloise, lean in to say something to her. She smiled prettily and twisted to face him. Ricky missed his next shot.

Whatever she'd said made Kyle laugh. He reached across her, grabbed the pitcher of beer and refilled both their glasses.

"Your shot."

He spun to face Jonathan. "Sorry."

"I know it must be boring to never lose and have to play every challenger, but at least pretend it's hard to beat me."

He laughed and lined up his shot, but just as he slid the stick forward Eloise's laughter floated to him. He missed.

"Are you doing this on purpose?"

He ran his hand along the back of his neck. "No. I'm distracted."

Jonathan followed the line of his gaze and laughed. "You're not jealous, are you?"

"Of course not." They were in an arrangement. The fact that Kyle had outgrown his geekiness, fit into his sweater and had hair that could have been on an infomercial for workout videos meant nothing.

Jonathan put his next three balls into the pockets with ease. "I'm getting confidence from your jealousy."

"I'm not jealous."

Eloise's giggle reached him again. He nearly cursed. Not because he was jealous. He couldn't be jealous. Refused to be. He was worried about their charade.

He put his stick on the table. "You win, Jon. You play the next challenger."

"But everybody wants to beat you. Geez, you're no fun when you have a girlfriend."

Ricky heard Jon's words, but they barely penetrated. He was focused on his date, who was currently being chatted up by one of his friends.

"Hey, *sweetie*," he said as he ambled up to the table.

She looked up at him with bright, happy eyes and his stomach plummeted. He'd never been able to put that look in her eyes. But Kyle had.

"Hey!" She scooted her chair over and made room for a chair for him, which someone immediately provided. "Kyle was just telling me that his company is looking to hire a human resources director."

Ricky glanced at Kyle, who reddened guiltily. "Really? I thought you were just in start-up stages."

"We are," Kyle said defensively.

Which meant he didn't need an HR person for at least a year. He didn't have to say it. Kyle got the message.

"Think I'll go play pool with Jon."

Ricky found himself saying, "You do that," and then wondering why he had. He was not the type to get jealous. Ever. Eloise wasn't really his date. She was a cover. A symbol to let people know he was getting past his grief. So why was he behaving like a Neanderthal?

Eloise patted the chair beside her. "Have a seat."

Confusion buffeted him. The noise of the bar closed in on him, and the last thing he wanted was to be squeezed into a cluster of people.

"I want to go home."

He heard the words coming out of his mouth and almost couldn't believe he'd said them. He sounded like a petulant child.

But Eloise didn't argue. She smiled and rose.

He strode over to get their coats. He handed hers to her without looking at her.

As she slid into it, his fraternity brothers came over and said their goodbyes. When all his goodbyes were made, he waved good-naturedly at the women, who still sat at the table.

They waved back, but he knew what they were thinking. That he still couldn't handle being out. That he was defensive, a prima donna who wasn't even trying to get over his grief.

He and Eloise stepped out into the cool air and he stopped. "I forgot to call Norman."

She huddled into her coat. "Is he close enough to get here in a few minutes?"

"That's his job." He pulled out his cell phone, sent a text to Norman and shoved his hands into the pockets of his leather jacket. "You're supposed to like me. You shouldn't have been flirting with Kyle."

"The guy was talking about a job. Everybody at the table heard every word we were saying. Everybody could see we weren't flirting. He was offering me a job."

"A nonexistent job."

She huddled more deeply into her coat. "Well, I know that now that you embarrassed him."

He ran his hand over his face. Damn. He *had* embarrassed him. He'd made an ass of himself and embarrassed a friend.

He was definitely losing it. "You should still know better than to think a half-drunk guy at a party is legit."

"So in other words, I shouldn't believe the guys you'll be introducing me to at your other parties...oh, wait... the other people you've introduced me to haven't actually talked about jobs. They're only concerned with getting your attention."

Norman pulled up and she strode to the limo. She didn't wait for Norman to come around to the side, just opened the door herself.

Ricky raced up behind her. "It's the fact that they want my attention that may get you noticed."

She sniffed a laugh as she slid inside. Norman stood off to the right, waiting for Ricky to enter. Once he had, he closed the door.

"No one will ever notice me as long as you're around." She sighed, disgusted with herself for getting angry with him. But she was angry. She knew this relationship was fake, but after their discussion about Wayne, she felt he knew her. The real her. Plus, she'd promised herself she would help him enjoy the holiday.

Still, he was the one who had ruined this evening, not her. She shifted to the right. "Just forget it."

"No. If you have something to say, I want to hear it."

She sucked in a breath. As Christmas angels went, she was a failure. He was mad. She was mad. So maybe it was just time to end this thing.

"All right, you want the truth. You've already gotten a lot out of this deal. We've gone through almost half your parties, and I don't have anything to show for it. So I saw an opportunity with Kyle and I pounced."

He stared sullenly out the window. "You should have known what he told you was ridiculous."

"And I'm an idiot for falling for it. Great. Fine. Thanks. I get it."

She crossed her arms on her chest. They stayed silent until they reached her apartment building. When Norman opened the door, she slid out. He started to get out behind her, but she pushed him back inside.

"Norman heard our fight." She glanced at Ricky's driver. "Didn't you?"

The man in the dark suit and driver's hat winced.

"Which means he'll perfectly understand when I say I don't want your pigheaded behind walking me to my apartment."

Norman winced again.

She slammed the door on Ricky and ran into the building. Not slowing down at the steps, she took them two at a time, raced into her apartment and back to her bedroom.

The stress of the night had destroyed her. When she put her head on her pillow, tears slid off her eyelids and rolled down her cheeks.

It hadn't been easy remembering her marriage, Wayne

getting sick, his death. She'd bared her soul to Ricky, not expecting understanding, but in trust. And the way he thanked her was to tell her she was foolish.

Yeah. Duh. She already knew that.

CHAPTER FIVE

THE NEXT MORNING a series of sharp knocks woke Eloise and Laura Beth. Both ran to the door, shrugging into long fleece robes. Eloise got there first, looked through the peephole and saw a man holding flowers.

Without disengaging the chain lock, she opened the door a crack.

"Are you Eloise Vaughn?"

"Yes."

He set the tall vase on the hall floor. "These are for you." He turned to go.

Eloise fumbled with the chain lock. "Wait! I'll give you a tip."

The kid smiled. "Tip was included." With that he raced down the hall.

She cautiously opened the door and picked up the vase. Tissue paper covered the flowers to protect them from the cold. She ripped it off. A holiday bouquet—roses, white mums, tinsel and mistletoe—greeted her.

Laura Beth closed the door. "Wonder who they're from?"

She opened the card, smiled. "My fake date. He says our fight last night made everything look real."

Laura Beth huffed away. "And his billions of dollars make it possible for him to wake a florist at—" She squinted at the clock. "My God, it's not even five o'clock yet. And it's Sunday!"

"He also says I was right. He hasn't been fulfilling his end of the bargain. So he sent the flowers early to catch me before I planned my day. If I want him to, he'll send his driver to pick me up and take me to his condo, where we can redo my résumé and look over my options."

That stopped Laura Beth. "That's the most romantic thing I've ever heard a guy say."

Eloise laughed. Poverty certainly changed a woman's view of romance. "Yeah. Me too." But she shivered. She wasn't sure she was done being angry with him. And sometimes being with him made her feel like a selfish failure as a human being. He was hurting and he wouldn't even tell her why. But she needed a job—so desperately needed a job—that maybe it was time to forget being a Christmas angel and just go back to their original deal.

She texted the number he'd put on the card and told him to send Norman. Then she found a copy of her résumé and got dressed.

Forty minutes later the driver texted her that he was downstairs, and she raced out into the cold, cold morning.

Norman held open the door. "Good morning, ma'am."

Eloise smiled. "Good morning, Norman."

He closed the door, got behind the wheel and sped off.

Surprise made her frown when he stopped the limo at a respectable but far from plush condo building. She rode up the normal elevator to a very normal hallway and knocked on a simple door.

Ricky opened the door immediately, as if he'd been waiting for her. "I am so sorry."

She tried to smile, but being in his presence sent shivers down her spine. In a sweater and jeans, he looked gorgeous and approachable, making it difficult to remember they were from two different worlds. Worse, they didn't seem to get along. She shouldn't be attracted to him.

She shrugged out of her navy blue parka. "Your flowers said it, but helping me find a job would say it even better."

As he took her coat to a convenient closet, she glanced around. Dark wood cabinets dominated the kitchen of the small open-plan condo and matched the dark table and chairs that took up the space before the living room.

"Have you eaten?"

She faced him. "No. But I'm not hungry."

"You had one piece of pizza last night. Not enough to sustain you." He walked into the kitchen and pulled a griddle from a lower cabinet. "I'm making pancakes."

Himself? She almost smiled. "Where's your maid?"

"She went with the penthouse."

"You lost your penthouse and maid? Was it a bet? A poker game?"

"I *sold* the penthouse and she chose to stay with the new owner. Which is only right because there's not a whole hell of a lot of housecleaning to do around here. This condo's tiny."

She liked his apartment, but she wouldn't trade a penthouse for it. "Why did you sell your penthouse?"

He spared her a glance. "I didn't need that much space." He paused and pulled in a breath before he added, "I also wanted to be alone."

She didn't have to be a mind reader to conclude that he'd sold his penthouse and gotten rid of his maid after his tragedy. This was as close as he'd ever come to telling her something personal. So she appreciated the gesture, sort of a peace offering, and said, "Well, this is nice. Modern. Kind of bacheloresque."

"Bacheloresque?"

"I made it up. It's a word meaning like something a bachelor would own."

He laughed as he gathered milk and eggs from the stainless steel refrigerator.

"You're making pancakes from scratch?"

"No. I've got a box mix, but it allows me to add fresh ingredients so they taste better."

It made sense to her, and she totally agreed a short while later when she took her first bite. "These are great."

He smiled, and they ate their pancakes amid sporadic conversation about the food, the condo and the cold. She wanted to ask him so many things, especially because he knew so much about her. But now that they were back to being congenial acquaintances with a mission, she knew better than to breach boundaries, poke or prod. She wanted a job. He wanted to help her find one. And her Christmas mission? He seemed to like her best when she wasn't trying to make him happy. So maybe it was time to scrap that.

He cleaned up, rinsing the dirty dishes and putting them into the dishwasher. Then they took mugs of coffee into the room he called his den.

Obviously designed to be a second bedroom, the small space barely had room for the big table with the huge computer system with three oversize screens, two keyboards and three printers. "Wow."

"I design games and think up extraspecial search engines," he said as he hit the button that turned everything on. Lights blinked, screens flashed, small motors hummed. "Did you bring your résumé?"

She pulled the folded sheet out of her jeans pocket.

He frowned. "I hope you don't send it out like that?"

The implication that she wasn't smart enough to send a neat résumé sent anger rumbling through her again. But looking around and remembering some of his conversations with his peers, she finally realized he might be one of those guys who was so intelligent he didn't think before he spoke.

Still, she wasn't going to let him get away with dissing her. "I'm not a dingbat. I print a fresh one every time I answer a classified ad or get a lead."

He sat at the desk, scanned her résumé and brought it up on a screen. He read for a few seconds, then said, "I think your first mistake is that you emphasize the secretarial aspects of your temp jobs." He faced her. "You'd be better off to list the jobs without giving too much explanation of what you actually do. That way you're accounting for the time, proving that you're working and not a slacker, but taking the emphasis off those skills, so people realize you're looking for a job that uses your degree."

She nodded.

Without asking for input, he revised her résumé, making it incredibly short, but also focusing on the skills she'd acquired while earning her degree.

Then he wrote a generic email introducing her and sent the email off to four friends with a copy of her updated résumé attached.

"These guys all owe me a favor. Your résumé will go directly to them."

Blissful hope ricocheted through her. "That'll get me a job?"

"Trust me. Two of them owe me favors big enough that if they can find you a job in your field within their companies, you'll get it. Hiring a friend of someone you owe is an easy way to pay off big favors."

Her heart lifted. But in the room filled with technology, he looked alone. She studied his solemn eyes, wishing she could fulfill her private vow to make him happy. But ever since she'd decided to make his Christmas wonderful, they'd actually become tenser around each other. They'd even fought.

Of course, he'd also sent her flowers and made her pancakes. And now he was trying in earnest to get her a job. To fulfill his part of the bargain. Early in the morning, as if he'd been so upset with himself he hadn't slept.

Something prickled inside her heart. A nudge or a hint that she shouldn't give up. A nice guy was inside him somewhere, a guy who had obviously been hurt. A guy who deserved a happy Christmas.

Deciding it was smarter not to wreck their current peace, she rose from the chair beside his. "Thanks."

He stood, too. "You're welcome."

Ridiculous silence enveloped them again. They weren't really dating. Technically, they weren't even friends. Hell, if she was going to get technical, they didn't actually know each other. So a vacuum existed. A couple saying good-bye would kiss. Friends saying goodbye might hug. People who were nothing to each other had nothing to do but be awkward.

She picked up her mug, chugged the now-cold coffee and grimaced. "Ugh."

He sniffed a laugh. "Cold coffee is disgusting."

"I know, but I was looking for one last swallow of warmth before I went outside."

He frowned. "I have more coffee. Or if you want, I can make you a cup of cocoa before you go."

She'd turned to leave, but the offer surprised her so much that she stopped. She *knew* that deep down inside Ricky Langley was a nice guy. And maybe he'd offered her cocoa because he didn't want her to go. Maybe, if she stayed, he'd open up to her.

She faced him with a cautious smile. "I like cocoa."

"Good."

He led her to his compact kitchen and pressed a button. The appliance garage door rose and a shiny stainless steel one-cup coffeemaker appeared. She sighed with appreciation. "It's beautiful."

He laughed. "And I happen to have some of the very best cocoa." He glanced back. "From Switzerland."

She peered over his shoulder. "Yum."

The cocoa took seconds to brew. He handed her the mug, then made a cup for himself.

Drink in hand, he pointed toward the seating area in the living room. "No sense standing while we drink this."

As she followed him, nerves settled in. They'd been

going to parties for two weeks, barely speaking except in a crowd of his friends and only discussing general topics. Unless he decided to open up immediately, they had nothing to talk about. No small talk to ease him into confiding.

Sitting on the chair, she noticed that some of the casual sculptures on his end tables and mantel weren't exactly as "casual" as he displayed them. And most were works from some of Olivia's clients.

She smiled. Something for them to talk about.

"I'm guessing Olivia helped you choose some of your art."

"She's persistent."

"And good at her job."

He laughed. "Yes."

She sipped her cocoa. The chocolate flavor that burst on her tongue made her groan. "This is fantastic."

He nodded, then said, "You and Olivia must be very close."

"That's what happens when you share an apartment. We've been together since university."

"That's right. Olivia's from Kentucky, too."

"And so is Laura Beth."

"So you're like the Three Musketeers?"

She shrugged. "I guess. We've gotten each other through some tough times."

"Your husband's illness?"

She shook her head and looked down at her cocoa. Hoping he was using talking about her to ease himself into talking about his tragedy, she said, "No. I was alone for that. Although Laura Beth, Olivia and I grew up in the same small town, we ran in different circles. When I went back to university to finish my degree, we found each other." She peeked up. Not knowing how much of her story Olivia had shared, Eloise cautiously said, "Olivia had had something traumatic happen to her and my experiences seemed to help nurse her back to sanity."

"She identified with your loss?"

She shook her head. It was good for them to have something to talk about to ease him into sharing his story, but she wouldn't talk at the expense of Olivia's privacy. Carefully crafting her answer, she said, "She identified more with being persecuted and abandoned."

"You were persecuted and abandoned?"

She caught his gaze. If he was going to ease himself in, shouldn't he have done it by now? Still, he already knew about Wayne. What did it matter to go a step or two further?

"Sort of. My parents disowned me."

"What?"

"My parents have money. I had rebelled. Embarrassed them by marrying someone so far below their class. So they kicked me out."

"Oh."

Great. Now, to him, she wasn't just a stupid girl. She was a stupid girl who was alone.

Fury with herself rattled through her. She never should have accepted the cocoa.

But she had. And she'd started a story that made her look bad. Again. She was just plain tired of looking bad to him, especially because this part of her problem wasn't her fault; it was her parents'. And call her prideful, but once, just once, she'd like to look sane to him.

"Even though they'd disowned me, when Wayne died I went home with my tail between my legs, expecting a scolding and probably a time of penance but also expecting to be accepted back. And maybe getting some help with my grief. Some love. But my parents wouldn't let me in." She shook her head. "They didn't even come to the door. A maid told me to leave and never come back."

He stared at her. "You had told them your husband had died, right?"

"They could not have cared less." She sighed. "I lost

my family because I married a guy I loved when I was too young to realize all the consequences. And every year, especially at Christmas, I mourn the loss. Not just of my husband, but also of my family. Olivia and Laura Beth go home, and I have nowhere to go. No home. It hurt to be rejected. It hurt not having their emotional support. But it's the aftermath of my mistakes that are killer. Years of loneliness. Years of regret. Getting kicked out of my family means I have no family. I have no one. I am alone."

She combed her fingers through her hair. She'd gone too far. Said things she didn't even admit to herself. And he was silent. He wasn't going to confide, and he didn't sympathize. He made no move to comfort her. She'd finally vocalized the thing she hadn't even told Laura Beth and Olivia, and he sat there, saying nothing.

And it all started because she'd been stupid enough to think he would open up to her.

Man, she was a goof. Or she didn't know very much about men. Or she didn't know much about rich men. But this guy who so easily found all her secrets, and got her to confess the rest, wasn't about to tell her anything.

She bounced off her seat. "You know what? Sunday is our cleaning day. I've got to get back to the apartment."

He rose. "Sure."

He walked to his closet, extracted her coat and helped her into it. "Let me call Norman to drive you."

She faced him. "Yeah, thanks. I'd appreciate that."

He pulled his phone out of his jeans pocket and texted. "He'll be downstairs in a second."

"Thanks."

Horrible awkwardness once again enveloped them as they stood in his entryway, humiliation cascading from her head to her toes. Why would she think he would confide in her? And why did she think he should care about her troubles? He didn't like her. She was a fake date. He'd helped her with her job search because that was his part of the bargain. Not because he liked her.

And she was an adult. She might not have a family, but she had good friends in Laura Beth and Olivia. Soon she'd have a job. She wasn't really *alone*. She was just alone on Christmas.

She sent him her fake smile. "I really appreciate this."

"You're welcome…again."

She winced. "I already said thanks, didn't I?"

"Yeah. You did."

Again, the little foyer grew quiet, and she suddenly realized why this awkwardness felt different, stronger. She had no reason to be standing there.

She was such an idiot. Always an idiot.

She turned to the door and, a gentleman, he reached around her to open it.

She slipped outside and headed down the silent, empty hall to the elevator. When would she learn none of this was real?

Ricky stood in front of the closed door, filled with pain for her. As she'd told him her story, it had taken every ounce of restraint he had not to pull her into his arms and comfort her.

But to what end? He was wounded as badly, if not worse than she was. She needed someone strong, someone whole, to be whole for her, to fill her stocking at Christmas and tell her it didn't matter that her parents didn't want her… She had him.

Yearning rose in him. How he wanted to do that. Wanted to give her that. She'd cared for a husband with cancer. She'd nursed him. She'd probably watched him die. Her parents had abandoned her. Rejected her in her hour of need.

Then she'd moved to New York City and found nothing but failure and more rejection.

He understood what it was like to be alone. Still, even

in his darkest hours, he knew he could pick up the phone and call his mom and dad.

She had no one. Any scrap of consolation or comfort could fill her. But he didn't have anything to give. He couldn't be a boyfriend for real.

So he'd kept his hands at his sides, measured his words, hadn't given her false hope.

Now he ached for her.

The next day, he went to work carrying the ache, trying to console himself with the reminder that he'd done something good for her when he'd gone the extra mile, brought her to his home and sent out her résumé. But it didn't work. The ache stayed with him. It sometimes even nudged aside the guilt he felt over Blake's death.

Somebody, somewhere had to really help this woman. Not just be a roommate or listen to her troubles, but do something tangible. And finding her a job suddenly seemed like the salvation she needed and also the way for him to feel better.

His secretary came into his office with that day's mail. "Good morning, Mr. Langley."

"Just set the mail on my desk—"

He stopped himself. He knew he was upset about Eloise, but that had sounded gruff and rude.

"I'm sorry. I shouldn't have snapped at you."

Halfway to the door, Janey paused. Peered back at him. "It's fine."

"No. I shouldn't have snapped. It's just that I had a weird weekend."

She took the few paces that brought her to his desk. "Are you okay?"

"Yes. Why?"

She shook her head. "You've never said you were sorry before." She smiled. "Never mind. Not important."

She left the room, and he didn't think anything of it until his personal assistant forgot to ship his mother's Christmas gift and he exploded. "It's Christmas season! Holiday mail is a mess. It takes weeks to get a parcel delivered. You can't—"

Thoughts of Eloise rumbled through him. Her parents wouldn't even accept gifts from her. He had parents who loved him. They not only loved his presents; they sent him presents also. They wanted him home for Christmas. They wanted him home anytime. Any day. It was his own sadness and guilt that kept him away.

Why was he shouting over something so trivial?

He ran his hand along the back of his neck. "I'm sorry. I'm sure if you get it out today, it will be fine."

David, his gray-haired assistant, nodded. "Okay. I'll get right on it."

"Great."

David started toward the door but stopped and turned around. "You didn't need to apologize. I don't take it personally when you yell. I know that's how you are."

"How I am?"

"Sometimes you talk loud. I'm accustomed to it. It doesn't bother me."

David left his office. Ricky walked to the window and blew his breath out on a sigh.

Sometimes he talked loud?

Sheesh. Was he a grouch? A Grinch? Somebody who yelled so much people thought it abnormal when he didn't?

Thoughts of Eloise shamed him. She was alone, yet never once had he seen her bite anyone's head off. Even when they'd argued after his frat party, she'd been reasonable.

He sighed. He didn't like discovering he was a grouch. Especially because he wasn't. He was sad about his son. Lonely for his son. And everyone understood that.

He sat down and squeezed his eyes shut. He remembered Blake's one and only Christmas. He could hear the sound of his little boy's laugh. See wrapping paper strewn on the floor. Remember the way Blake loved cookies, chattered nonsensical baby words with Ricky's mom, sat on his dad's lap.

He swallowed.

If he was grouchy with his staff over missing Blake, over feeling guilty about Blake's death, he had a right. Even his staff knew that.

Feeling sorry for a woman he barely knew? It didn't make sense. Her making him feel bad for something he had no right to be guilty about? Well, that didn't make any sense either. Why should a woman he barely knew affect him like this?

He had to fix it. The best way would be to get his relationship with Eloise back to where it was supposed to be.

A deal.

Not a friendship, and certainly not a romance.

Simply a deal.

He didn't hear anything from the CEOs he'd sent her résumé to, and by Wednesday that bothered him. Once he got her a job, everything between them would balance out, and they could go back to being strangers pretending to date. So no response annoyed him. Still, his friends might not have called *him* because *she* was the one who wanted the job.

Given that it was Wednesday, the day before their next party—so he needed to call her with the information about that weekend's events—he picked up his phone. He wouldn't interrogate her, but if the subject of interviews came up, he wouldn't waste it.

"I wanted to let you know that Thursday's party is formal again."

"Oh. Okay. Good."

He winced, waiting for her to mention if she'd gotten calls from his friends, if she'd gotten interviews. When twenty seconds passed in silence, he sighed. "You didn't hear from my friends, did you?"

"No."

"Which means you didn't get a job."

"Nope."

Annoyance with his friends buffeted him. But sorrow for her sneaked in there too. This woman could not get a break. Still, he had troubles of his own. Guilt of his own. Shame of his own. A baby boy he missed so much sometimes his chest ached. He had enough trouble without getting involved with her and her problems. He had to help her find a job, but he couldn't get personally involved.

Needing to get them back to their deal and get himself out of this conversation, he said, "Even if someone hires you, the deal is twelve dates for a job. Not you get a job, then you quit." He grimaced, even more frustrated with himself. In trying to keep his distance, he'd made himself look like a grizzly bear. "I didn't mean that to sound as grouchy as it did."

She sighed. "I know."

He grimaced again. He almost told her how he'd noticed ten thousand times in the past three days how surly he was. How difficult he was to deal with. He knew it was the result of losing a child. And suddenly, he longed to tell someone. To share his pain. Or maybe he longed to tell her because he knew she'd understand?

But all he said was, "Good."

"So you want me to wear a gown."

"Yes." He paused. "Do you want me to make follow-up calls with the guys I sent your résumé to?"

"You can do that?"

"They are my friends. But they also owe me."

Silence greeted him. Finally she said, "Although I appreciate the offer, I still have some pride. I'd like to get a job based on my qualifications."

"You really don't have many."

"Thanks."

Damn it. He might not want to confide in her, but there

was no reason to hurt her. He slapped his desk. "See? There I go again. I have no filter on my tongue when it comes to business, and sometimes I'm just a little too honest."

"I think your honesty is your best quality."

He winced. "Tell my employees that."

"Why do you think your friends come to you for advice?"

"Because I tell them the truth?"

"Sometimes brutally."

He laughed, then marveled that he'd laughed even though he continually said the wrong thing. Even though he couldn't stop thinking about Blake. Even though he had guilt that swallowed him whole some days, she kept making him laugh and he kept making her miserable. "Let me call my friends."

"No. I don't want to be that girl in the office who only got her job because of her boyfriend. It's why I didn't want a job from you. I can't be the girl in the office who only got her job because her boyfriend pulled strings."

It wasn't so much what she said but how she said it that caused him to shake his head. "It's been a long time since anybody called me a boyfriend."

"Fake or not, that's what you are." She settled onto the wide sill of her living room window, wishing, like Binnie Margolis, for snow. Laura Beth was out. Olivia was in Kentucky. Christmas was getting close. Telling her story to Ricky on Sunday morning had pounded home the fact that she'd soon be facing another holiday by herself, without even a blanket of snow to make her feel cozy in her empty apartment with her eighteen-inch plastic tree and the cookies Olivia's mom would mail to her.

She swallowed. Desperate to get her mind off her troubles, she said the first thing that popped into her head. "So how was your day?"

He sniffed. "Same. Kinda boring."

"Really? Rich wheeler-dealer like you has boring days?"

He hesitated, as if he really didn't want to talk anymore, but he said, "It was fun when I started out. Now things are routine."

"Maybe you need a new venture."

"A new venture?"

"You know. Instead of writing new video games, invent a different kind of microwave popcorn. Try taking that to market. I'll bet you'll meet some challenges."

He laughed. "Microwave popcorn?"

"Hey, my dad loves the stuff..." Even as the words flipped out of her mouth, her heart tugged. Her stomach plummeted. As gruff and socially conscious as her parents were, they were her family and they didn't want her.

How could she miss people who didn't want her around?

Her eyes filled with tears. "I'm sorry. Someone's knocking on the door. I've gotta run. See you Thursday night. In a gown."

She didn't wait for his reply, just clicked off, tossed her phone to the sofa and laid her head on her knees. She refused to be pathetic, refused to let tears fall for the loss of people who didn't want her. She'd done that enough in her twenty-five years. All she wanted was a job, a way to support herself. And once she got it, she'd be fine.

She repeated that mantra as she went to bed, got up, showered, dressed for work, jumped on the subway, rode up in the average elevator to the law office and made coffee for the senior partners, none of whom even acknowledged her existence.

CHAPTER SIX

THURSDAY NIGHT RICKY walked up the four flights of stairs to Eloise's apartment, trepidation riding his blood. Every Christmas decoration reminded him of his son. Even the cold air reminded him of bundling Blake in a snowsuit, buying knit caps.

Wanting to roll up in a ball of misery and privately mourn Blake, he was tempted by thoughts of ending this charade. He could bow out of the rest of the parties. All he had to do was go to Jamaica or Monaco, and everybody would be jealous of his vacation. Nobody would wonder why he wasn't attending any more of the parties.

Except Eloise didn't have a job. Taking her to these events was his best way of keeping her in front of his friends who might want to hire her. Lord knows, sending emails hadn't worked.

Not sure what he'd find when she came to the door, he sucked in a breath before he knocked. When the door opened, she stood before him looking beautiful in a simple straight gown. Red and shiny, it complimented her hair, which she'd put in some curly creation on top of her head and spun thin tinsel through.

"You look great." The words popped out naturally, and he almost shook his head in wonder that just seeing her had him feeling better.

When she smiled, relief poured through him. It would

have been a long night if she'd been as depressed as she had been on Sunday morning and in their phone call. Instead, she'd pulled herself together. He admired that.

He returned her smile. "Every dress gets better."

She laughed as she handed him her black cape. "That's because the closer we get to the actual holiday, the more Christmas-y I feel. Just wait till you see what I'm pondering for Christmas Eve."

They walked to the limo and, when Norman opened the door, they slid in. With the advanced stage of the season, more and more shops and apartment windows were decorated for the holiday. Bright lights winked. Tinsel blew in the bitter breezes. Because it was cold, everything had a sparkly, icy look, but it wasn't quite as pretty as if there had been snow.

"I like snow too."

He spun to face her. Had he said that out loud? "I…um… grew up near the Finger Lakes." Damn. So much for trying not to be personal. "By now, they're probably knee-deep in the white stuff."

"Probably? You don't know?"

He peeked at her. "If there's snow?"

She nodded.

He winced. "I haven't talked to my parents in a while."

She said, "Oh. Okay," as if she understood. And he supposed if anybody understood complicated relationships with parents, it would be her.

But that only reminded him of how difficult her life was, and when she turned away from him, that ridiculous sadness for her filled him again. Fighting it, he squeezed his eyes shut. She would be fine. Once he helped her land a job, she'd be ecstatic. He did not have to feel sorry for her.

They walked into the hotel, and he dropped off their outerwear at the coat check. Just before they entered the ballroom, he saw her shift her face and change her countenance. She formed a smile big enough to remove the sad expression in her eyes, but he saw no light in them. Then she slid her hand in the crook of his elbow and they walked into the ballroom.

Guilt buffeted him. She was going the whole nine yards for him and he wasn't really doing anything for her.

Seated with another group of his friends, he held out her chair as he made quick introductions, and the discussion immediately zoomed to stock options.

This was why he'd never worried that anyone at any of the parties they attended would tell Eloise about Blake. His friends didn't talk about anything but business. And the wives who didn't join in on the discussion of stocks and strategies generally sat dutifully at the husbands' sides or chatted among themselves about inconsequential, party-worthy topics, not ridiculously sad things that would bring everybody down. He wasn't saying they were fake. They were more like courteous. Proper.

Still, with his mission in mind, he tried to work human resources into the conversation but couldn't. Frustration wound through him. No wonder Eloise couldn't find a job. No one seemed to care about the administration of their projects. All they cared about was the project itself.

When the dancing started, he and Eloise moved to the dance floor. He slid his hand across the smooth material covering her back. Attraction slithered through him. With every inch of his heart and soul, he longed to pull her to him and just give her what she needed. A little bit of affection. But although he might be able to hug her tonight, maybe kiss her, who knew what he'd be like tomorrow? And if he held her tonight, kissed her tonight and then couldn't get out of bed the next day because of debilitating grief… wouldn't he hurt her?

Yes. He would. And he refused to do that to her.

Needing to get his mind off how good she felt, he said, "So this is a pretty nice party."

She met his gaze and smiled. "They're all wonderful."

"I'm glad you enjoy them."

"I do."

His conscience tweaked again. While he took all this for granted, she was happy to get a good meal and a nice glass of wine, even though he basically ignored her. With the exception of dancing, he was generally occupied with his friends, and when he wasn't, his fear of getting too close kept him from really talking to her.

"Even with a grouch like me?"

She laughed lightly. "Oh, you're not so bad."

But he was. He knew he was. Ever since she'd told him about being alone and made him realize he had an abundance of things to be thankful for, he'd seen the signs. Short temper with his staff. Nothing but cool professionalism with Norman. Presents for his friends and his family bought by David. Hell, he didn't even know what he'd bought his own mother for Christmas. Since Blake's death, he'd insulated himself inside a bubble of sadness. He didn't think that was wrong, but he did see he was letting Eloise down. He'd made a promise that he couldn't seem to keep. And suddenly it became overwhelmingly important that he at least do something for her, even if it was only make her happy for one night.

"We should do tequila shots."

She laughed and pulled back so she could see his face. "What?"

He'd surprised himself as much as her with the suggestion. But now that he'd said it, it sort of made sense.

"Tequila shots. This party might be nice, but we've gone to six of these. They're getting boring. Tequila shots would liven up this place."

Another laugh spilled out of her, causing his heart to tug and his chest to tighten with something that felt very much like pride that *he'd* made *her* laugh for a change.

"I'm sure the hosts would be thrilled."

"Why not? Isn't the purpose of giving a party to make your friends happy?"

"Yes." She said the word slowly, as her eyes rose, and she met his gaze. Soft but curious, the light in her crystal blue orbs told him she was cautious about the shots, but the idea appealed to her.

Pleasure rolled through him. He spun her around, mentally thanking Tucker Engle for forcing him to take ballroom dancing classes so he wouldn't be awkward at these parties. Not only had it turned out that he loved to dance, but tonight he loved seeing that light in her eyes.

"So, if we asked the bartender to set up shots, maybe eighteen or twenty, we could probably get that many people to join us. I'll bet with every shot, our crew would grow."

"Our crew? Are you nuts?" She shook her head, but her eyes glowed.

He spun her around again. "Maybe. But I see at least three of my fraternity brothers. I'll bet we could have this place rocking in three shots."

She laughed gaily. "I'll bet you'd have a room full of drunks in three shots."

"But think of the pictures that would show up in tomorrow's society pages."

She laughed and shook her head. "It would probably be the newspaper's best issue ever."

The music stopped and, as always, one of his friends slid over. After introductions, he asked Ricky a question about a company he was considering partnering in and, as Ricky answered, his gaze slid to Eloise.

She stood at his side, smiling, playing the part. But they never touched. Aside from when they danced. Or when *she* put her hand in the crook of his elbow. Or when *she* fixed his bow tie.

He'd never touched her with affection. Never held her hand. Never put his arm around her. To a woman who lived her life without family, without affection, his lack of touch probably seared her.

He reached out and took her hand. Her gaze swung to his. He smiled. She smiled. He tugged her closer. And while they held hands, his conversation continued until the band began to play again.

This time when he pulled her into his arms, he felt her relax against him. He relaxed a little himself. He wasn't making this real. Just realistic. And, all right, he also wanted her to feel wanted. He might only need her to help him get through the holiday. But he *needed* her, which meant he *wanted* her around.

And she needed to know that somebody wanted her. Albeit for a little while.

When the band took a break, he walked her to their table, then excused himself. When he returned, he had two shots of tequila. She burst out laughing. Their table-mates frowned.

He nodded at the shots, as he sat by Eloise. "Private joke."

He picked up a shot and motioned for her to do the same. "Ready?"

"I think this is kinda nuts."

"It's been a long, hard couple of years for both of us. Maybe one night of I-don't-care is in order."

"One night of I-don't-care?"

"One night of forgetting everything and just having a good time."

She picked up her shot. "I could handle that."

They downed the tequila. She shuddered in distaste but laughed, and when the band began to play again, they were both more comfortable.

The music shifted to a quiet, mellow tune, and he pulled her into his arms for a slow dance. She melted against him. Loose from the tequila, he rested his chin on the top of her head and inhaled the fragrance of her hair. For the first time in eighteen months, he just let go.

When the band took a break, they took another shot and washed it down with a glass of champagne. Dancing took a lot of the sting out of the alcohol. Still, by the time they returned to her apartment, they were just tipsy enough to clamor up the stairs.

The "shh" she sent back to him from the step above his only made him laugh.

When they stopped in front of her apartment door, she said, "We're gonna get me kicked out of my building."

He put his hands on her shoulders. He wasn't one for medicating pain with alcohol, but tonight wasn't about getting rid of pain. It had been about acknowledging it and telling it to go to hell for a few hours.

"If I get you kicked out of your building, I'll find you another apartment."

She snorted a laugh. "Laura Beth and I can barely afford the one we have."

Her words slurred endearingly. He smiled stupidly. "I had a good time."

"So I'm guessing you're thinking we should have tequila shots at every party."

"Well, we wouldn't want to form any bad habits, but..." He glanced around, searching his alcohol-numbed brain for the words that should follow that *but*, and in the end he couldn't help stating the obvious. "It was good to loosen up a bit. I really had fun."

She put her hands on his chest. "Doesn't happen for you much, does it?"

He shook his head. "Doesn't happen at all."

"So, I'm good for you."

She was. When her life didn't make him feel like an ingrate, she was. Thinking of her, instead of himself, instead of his grief, instead of his guilt, was so much easier.

The urge to kiss her swam through his blood, making it

tingle. But it was the very fact that he was so tempted that stopped him. She was good for him. But he wasn't good for her. He was broken. She was broken, too. But that meant she needed someone strong, someone filled with love to shower her with affection. And that wasn't him.

He stepped back. "Good night, Eloise."

"Do you realize that's the first time you've said my name?"

"I say your name all the time."

"Yeah, when you introduce me." Her gazed locked with his. "But you've never said it to me."

The urge to kiss her shimmied through him again. She was so pretty, so perfect. So wonderful sometimes. And thanks to Preston he knew her lips were as soft as a cloud, the inside of her mouth like silk.

He took a step closer.

She put her hands on his lapels again and slid them up his chest.

Need surged. Not just from the intimacy of her touch, but from hope. He longed for her to put her hands around his neck, something she didn't do in their very proper dancing. He yearned for her to hold him. To hug him. To pull him close.

Instead, she straightened his tie and smiled up at him.

She wouldn't make the first move, but she clearly was telling him she wanted him to kiss her.

Desire pleaded with him. *Just do it. Just bend your head. Just kiss her.*

His breath faltered. Dear God, he wanted this.

But he knew himself. When the tequila wore off, he'd regret it. And even if he didn't, he'd leave her. Not in a big, splashy departure scene. But after these parties, he'd stop calling. He'd drift back to his own dark, quiet world because his guilt wouldn't let him handle the bright optimistic world she wanted. And he'd forget her.

He would hurt a woman who'd been hurt enough.

He closed his fingers around her hands and removed them from his lapel. "Good night, Eloise."

Then he turned and walked away, his mouth yearning for a kiss, his limbs longing to hold her, his heart telling him he was a fool.

Ten o'clock the next morning, Eloise's pride could no longer hold off the pounding in her head. She rose from her desk and walked into the employee break room, where she rifled through the cabinet above the sink until she found painkillers.

Getting water from the cooler beside the refrigerator, she glanced up sharply when Tina Horner walked in with her empty mug and ambled to the coffeemaker.

"What's up?"

"Nothing." She popped the two pills into her mouth, chugged her water and headed for the door and up the hall to her office. She and Tina weren't supposed to leave their cabinets full of confidential files unattended. A fact Tina frequently forgot…or ignored…because she was a full-time employee with little fear of being fired or replaced.

A few seconds later, Tina caught up with her. "Come on. You can't tell me nothing's wrong. I've worked beside you for weeks. You never need painkillers."

"Ricky and I went to a party last night."

Tina's face glowed with curiosity. "Another formal one?"

"Yep."

"On a Thursday?"

"Rich people don't need to keep the same schedule you and I do. I'm guessing if there's a party on Thursday, they don't work on Friday."

Tina took the left at the hall that led to their office. "So while you're here nursing a hangover, your date's probably still in bed?"

"Yep." But now that she thought about it, she doubted it. She'd never met anybody with the work ethic Ricky had.

Plus, he had enough technology in his den that he could work in his pajamas. The thought made her laugh.

Tina narrowed her eyes at her. "So add a hangover to a silly laugh, and I'm guessing you had a really good time last night."

She slipped into their office and over to her desk. "Yes. I had a good time."

Tina sat and eyed Eloise. "Let's see... What is it you aren't telling me?" She tapped her index fingers on her cheeks. "You drank too much. You probably also danced a lot." Her expression grew thoughtful. "But you've been doing that all along." She considered that for another second, then her mouth fell open. "He kissed you good-night."

Getting to work, Eloise examined the files list on her screen and said, "I wish."

Tina gasped. She bounced from her chair and over to Eloise's desk. "Your fake dating has turned into real dating!"

Eloise shook her head. "I said I wish. I didn't say it happened." And because of how happy dancing snuggled against him had made her feel, the realist in her had wept with sadness when he'd walked away from that kiss. A chance to bond. A chance to express that their feelings were changing. A chance to actually be themselves.

And he'd walked away from it.

"You really like him, don't you?"

Eloise squeezed her eyes shut. Memories from the night before flooded her. The joy of simple human contact had morphed into happiness, which had shifted into an acknowledgment that she more than liked this guy. "Sometimes I think I might be falling in love with him."

"Oh, honey!" Tina leaned her hip on Eloise's desk. "It's one thing to want to kiss and feel like you're living a fairy tale with a rich guy. It's another to start believing it's real."

"I know."

"You're going to get your heart broken. And this isn't

going to be like whatever heartbreak you had in college that drove you to New York City."

Eloise frowned. "What makes you think getting my heart broken drove me to New York City?"

Rising from Eloise's desk, Tina laughed. "The sad look that doesn't often leave your eyes."

"I have a sad look?"

"Sort of like a lost puppy."

Her head swam. All this time she'd thought she was a rock of sanity, when she was giving off a sad look. "I look like a dog?"

"You look like somebody who needs a hug. You're a sweet, wonderful person. If someone gets to know you and like you, it's hard not to want to help you."

"People want to help me?"

"Not everyone." Tina returned to her desk and put her attention on her computer screen. "But it's not easy to watch you struggle every day. It makes me want to do something nice for you. If only bring you a doughnut."

She remembered the once-a-week doughnut Tina bought her and then thought of the conversation she'd had with Ricky before he'd suggested the shots. "Or tequila."

Tina peered around her computer monitor at Eloise. "Tequila?"

She shook her head. "Never mind." But mortification filled her. Ricky Langley had been seeing her "sad face" for weeks. And last night she'd been particularly sad. So, like Tina, he'd wanted to cheer her up. He wasn't falling for her. That was why he hadn't kissed her. He didn't want to get romantic. He just wanted her to stop her sadness.

What an idiot she was! No wonder she couldn't get a job. Her ability to read people and their actions was non-existent. And people looked at her and saw sadness. Not competence. Not reliability. *Sadness*.

She had to fix that.

* * *

Ricky got up late with no sign of a hangover. Smug, he showered, congratulating himself for remembering to hydrate before going to bed. But even as he had the thought, he wondered if Eloise had drunk enough water—

His heart stuttered. *Eloise.* He'd damn near kissed her the night before. Just the memory of that almost kiss put the need in his blood again, tightened his chest. He'd desperately wanted to kiss her, but he'd risen above it.

Thank God. Because he wasn't good for her. He lived in a world of guilt and sadness. He refused to bring her into that.

Norman arrived, and he got into the limo and tried to focus on that day's meetings, but he failed. Even thoughts of Blake drifted away when memories of laughing with Eloise filled his head. The noisy way they climbed up her stairway. Those thirty seconds he could have kissed her—

He frowned. He might have risen above the temptations of last night, but what about the next time?

The "next time" he'd be tempted wasn't a week away, time enough to shore up his defenses. Tonight they had another party. And he still had a tingle in his blood. A funny feeling that pressed into his heart every time he thought her name.

He groaned. She liked when he said her name. He liked saying her name. This was bad.

He entered the private elevator to his office suite.

He could handle the desire. That sweet need that nudged him to touch his lips to hers was a natural male urge. Especially with a woman as beautiful as Eloise. But that yearning to be held? The longing for connection that he'd nearly drowned in the night before? That was just wrong.

He didn't need connections. He didn't even *want* connections. Being alone was better for him. Then he didn't worry about snarling at his employees or insulting his friends.

Ever since he'd met Eloise, his entire life had kept getting confused. Even his work life.

He paused his thoughts. *That* was the real problem. She was drawing him back into the world again, as if he belonged there. She made him forget he had trouble in his life. But he did. He had troubles that wouldn't go away with a wave of a magic wand. He couldn't pretend they didn't exist.

He scrubbed his hand across his mouth. If he were smart, he'd have David call Eloise and tell her that her services were no longer needed. But they had made a deal, and he hadn't fulfilled his end of the bargain.

He couldn't back out. True leaders never reneged on deals. That was how otherwise-smart business professionals got bad names. He had to take her to the party that night. And every night until he found her a job.

Which meant holding her and talking to her.

He scrubbed his hand across his mouth again. If there was one thing he hadn't expected from this deal it was that he would like her. But, surely, he could get beyond that.

CHAPTER SEVEN

THAT NIGHT ELOISE wore a black gown paired with bright silver jewelry.

Feeling awkward and wishing he'd called and canceled, Ricky said, "As always, you look amazing."

She caught his gaze, her eyes searching his. He stood very still, very proper, under her scrutiny, hoping to make her believe it had been nothing but the tequila that had made him so affectionate the night before. That he didn't really want to kiss her. That he didn't really want anything from her except to finish their deal.

Eventually, she smiled slightly. "As always, you're good for my ego."

She handed him her cape, and, closing his eyes, he slid it on her shoulders, so relieved that she was handling this with grace and discretion that he couldn't even put the feeling into words.

But an unexpected urge hit him. His end of the deal was to help her find a job. Although that hadn't yet panned out, he would see to it that it did. And it would cost him nothing but a little time and effort.

But she spent every darned Friday and Saturday night with him. Not to mention a Thursday and some Sundays. Buying her an evening jacket, a fur, something better than her worn cape, wouldn't be out of line. To his bank account, it would be small token of appreciation. Just as going out with her had become difficult; going out with him couldn't be easy either. Yet she handled it like a trooper.

"I was actually thrilled to find a way to wear this jewelry."

Pulling himself out of his reverie, he realized they'd not only clattered down the four flights of stairs, but he'd missed a chunk of conversation. He opened the building door for her and she strolled outside.

"The jewelry looks nice with your dress."

She laughed. "Good evening, Norman."

He tipped his hat. "Ma'am."

They climbed inside. "You don't have to pretend you enjoy talking about jewelry."

"I don't mind." But he was clueless.

"I just sometimes get carried away." She sighed. "I love to dress up." She winced. "That makes me sound like a kid. I don't love to dress up as much as I love fashion. I love it when Olivia calls for advice." She paused, faced him. "You do know Olivia and Tucker will be at tonight's party."

That woke him up. "Really?"

"Yes. She called this morning, then texted pictures of two gowns. She almost wore something brown until I talked her into a beautiful red Vera Wang."

He struggled with a smile. He'd forgotten how goofy women could get about clothes. And tonight Eloise was particularly goofy, talking nonstop, as if she were trying to prove to him that she was fine. Happy. Not going to get hysterical on him because he wanted to pretend last night hadn't happened.

Appreciating that, he kept the conversation going. "That's a tragedy averted."

She playfully nudged his arm. "All right. All right. I get it. You think talking about clothes is silly."

Laughter bubbled through him. The kind he'd almost forgotten he existed. Teasing, we-don't-have-to-be-normal, merriment. "Tucker once called and asked for advice about his tux."

She laughed. "Stop."

"I said, 'Tucker, go with the bow tie.'"

She swatted him. "Stop!"

"He went with the regular tie and all night long everybody kept giving him funny looks."

"Stop!"

He laughed. "Sorry."

But to Eloise he didn't look sorry. He looked happy. The way he had when they were drinking tequila the night before. Three shots and some champagne hadn't nearly put him under the table as it had done to her. But it had certainly relaxed him. And it appeared his good mood wasn't gone.

She blanched remembering how she'd all but asked for a good-night kiss, and she was glad he'd not only walked away, but also seemed to have totally forgotten that she stood there wide-eyed, her lips parted, her brain chanting a litany hoping he'd telepathically get the message that he should kiss her.

Now that she knew he didn't like her—he only felt sorry for her—she absolutely wanted him to forget her begging for a kiss the night before. If it killed her, she intended to project happiness. No sad puppy-dog eyes, as Tina said. Just a normal woman at a party. With him still happy and with Olivia and Tucker around, that should be relatively easy.

As they got out of the limo at the Ritz, Ricky reached for her hand. His warm fingers wrapped around hers and her heart stumbled. All right, need-to-look-like-a-normal-woman aside, she desperately wanted to have another fun night. Another night when he was warm and natural. She would be alone on Christmas day. She needed good memories of these nights with him, nights when they laughed and had fun together, to think about when she played carols on her phone and tried not to remember she had no one in her life.

They met Tucker and Olivia in the lobby. Eloise hugged her pregnant friend, who, to a baby novice, felt extremely large around the middle. "I'm so glad you're home."

Tucker said, "We couldn't miss Fred Murphy's party."

His hand on the small of Olivia's back, Tucker headed for the elevator to the ballroom, and Ricky leaned down and whispered, "He was the first banker to give Tucker money."

She peeked up into his sleepy brown eyes, fighting the urge to believe his keeping her up-to-date with necessary information proved he liked her. Even though that might make her memories more interesting on Christmas Day, she didn't want to get carried away. As Tina had said, that was how women got their hearts broken. She just wanted to have a good time. Something to think about on Christmas morning.

"So all this fuss is about a loan?"

He shook his head. "An investment."

"Ah. Money he didn't have to pay back."

"Yes. But it was more the confidence he had in Tucker."

"I get it."

She and Ricky caught up to the Engles just as the elevator door opened. Eloise undid the buttons of her cape and Olivia gasped.

"So that's what you did with that big black ball gown?"

She laughed. "Hard to believe this used to have eight layers of tulle, isn't it?"

"It's stunning. I should be coming to you for my gowns."

"Oh, I don't know. That Vera Wang suits you very well."

Olivia glanced down at her red gown. "It is pretty."

"It's gorgeous."

Olivia shook her head. "Yeah, and I'm glad you talked me into it. You have such a talent for this stuff."

* * *

The discussion of gowns and sewing swirled around Ricky's head, and he almost laughed again at the silly conversation he and Eloise had had in the car. When he was with her, something about her always made him smile, and that wasn't good. When he was happy, he let his guard down and if he let his guard down too much, he'd kiss her. And if he started kissing her, he'd hurt her.

The opening of the elevator doors came as a grand relief, and they stepped out. Eloise handed Ricky her cape, and, as she turned, he saw the back of her dress.

Or lack thereof.

Walking to the coat check desk, he silently prayed for strength. She was making him laugh, forget himself and tease her. He was only human. With his attraction and sense of comfort with her, he kept inching closer and closer to the place where he wouldn't be able to resist kissing her. And tomorrow he'd regret it and pull back and probably hurt her.

He could not hurt her. No matter how hard he had to fight, he would do everything in his power to keep his distance.

Still, after dinner and the short, humorous awards ceremony Fred put on, he and Eloise were one of the first couples on the dance floor. Everyone knew he loved to dance, but, more than that, Tucker and Olivia were also here. As much as he wasn't the kind to fool his close friends, the charade was well under way. Despite fighting feelings for Eloise, he couldn't end their deal when he hadn't found her a job. And he couldn't tell his best friend that he wasn't really dating his wife's BFF, that it had been a bargain. They'd both look crazy.

So he pulled Eloise into his arms and she nestled against him. When her softness met his chest, he struggled with the desire to just close his eyes and enjoy.

He looked down. She looked up. Their gazes met in

acknowledgment of the fact that their tequila night had brought them closer. But he didn't want to be close. He wanted them to go back to being polite strangers who could pretend they liked each other.

So he pulled several inches away, putting enough space between them to retain his sanity. Still, every time they moved, his hand on the small of her back slid against her satiny skin. He remembered the sparkle in her eyes at her apartment door last night. How she'd wanted him to kiss her. How he'd longed to do just that.

But he also remembered that he was grieving his son, filled with guilt and remorse over his death. She had troubles of her own. Neither one was in a position to indulge an attraction that might end up hurting them both.

He held himself stiffly for the first set and was relieved when the band took a break. Eloise chatted with Olivia about her clients and art in general, and he and Tucker bounced around ideas about the stock market.

When the second set began, he was a little too tired to hold himself away from her. When she melted, his body tried to resist, but it was no use. Her breasts met his chest. Their thighs brushed as they moved to the music. His hormones awoke like a band of angels ready to sing the "Hallelujah Chorus."

"I don't think I've ever seen so many diamonds in my life."

Glad to get his mind off his hormones and also curious about where her mind had gone, he laughed. "Cumulatively or at this party?"

"It almost doesn't matter." She pulled back and looked at him. "Something odd has been striking me tonight."

With the feeling of the velvet skin of her back pressed against his hand, something had been striking him all night, too. He'd love to run his hand down her back just once. Just for the thrill of it.

But talking about that wouldn't do either one of them any good. So he smiled and politely said, "What's that?"

"My mom doesn't have a diamond necklace."

He bit out a laugh. "What?"

"Look at all these necklaces. Or just think about the one around Olivia's throat. Tucker adores his wife so he showers her with diamonds. That's how wealthy men show their love."

He smiled. "It is?"

"Sure. If you can't say the words, you buy a gift. A necklace. A bracelet. A fur."

His mouth twisted. He wanted to buy her a fur, but that didn't mean he loved her. "It's not always about love."

"True. It could be about respect or appreciation. You know, a thanks-for-putting-up-with-me gift."

He coughed. That was exactly why he wanted to buy her a fur. "You seem so sure."

"People are transparent. But none of this is actually my point."

"What's your point?"

"My mother doesn't have a diamond necklace."

"You think your dad doesn't love her or doesn't appreciate her?"

"I think he doesn't have hundreds of thousands to millions of dollars to spend on jewelry."

Ricky stopped dancing. Confused, he said, "Everybody here does."

"Which is the conclusion of my point." She nudged him to start dancing again. "My parents have lots of money. But they're not in this class."

He frowned, not quite understanding what she was getting at. "So?"

"So maybe that's why they were so mad that I embarrassed them."

He thought back to his beginnings in New York City society. He remembered renting a tux because he didn't own one and hiring a limo with a driver. He hadn't done it for the sake of impressing anyone. He simply wanted to fit in. Not look like an upstart. Not look like somebody who didn't belong. If Eloise's parents were image conscious, her embarrassing them might have shaken them more than normal people. That is, if they thought more of their station in society than their daughter. And it appeared they did.

"Maybe."

"The few times we came to New York City for Christmas events, they were extremely clear with me and my older brother that we shouldn't do anything to embarrass them."

He frowned, catching her gaze. "Where is all this coming from?"

She shrugged. "I did some thinking today. Came to some conclusions."

A happy thought filled him with hope. He might not have found her a job, but maybe being with him had caused her to see some things about her life, things that might help her stop being so sad.

"So the past couple of weeks with my friends has been good for you?"

She shook her head. "It doesn't matter."

He twirled them around. "Of course it matters. You miss your parents. You're trying to figure it out because you're trying to find an angle or reason to go home."

She glanced away. "I don't think so."

He desperately wanted her to be able to go home, to have the acceptance she needed. Not just to make sure she got something from their deal, but because no one should be alone for Christmas. Especially not somebody so pretty and so nice.

He waited a second, then said, "What would you have to do to be able to go home?"

She smiled devilishly. "Buy my mom a diamond necklace?"

He huffed out a sigh. "I'm being serious here."

"I don't think I can go home."

He glanced down. "Why not?"

She looked away for a few seconds, then caught his gaze again. "I've found more love and acceptance with Olivia and Laura Beth than I ever had with my parents. And with their acceptance I realized how dysfunctional my own family is."

He thought about how he hadn't been home in nearly two years. Didn't call. Didn't take his mother's calls. Because everything about his family reminded him of Blake.

"Everybody's family is dysfunctional to a degree."

"Not like this. My parents don't know how to love. Even though it hurts to have no one, sometimes a person is better off being alone than living around people who only use them."

Or sometimes a person is better off being alone than being with people who only revive their sorrow.

"Maybe."

"Okay, here's the best example. My parents would love to see me with you. They'd use that like a stepladder. They'd treat me like royalty to get to *you*. And then they'd use you for introductions or insider information or whatever they thought they could get. But when you and I stopped seeing each other, they'd put me back on a shelf again. Like something they pulled out when they needed it." She shook her head. "As a kid, when they'd put me back on the shelf, I'd jump through hoops to get their attention, their affection. I'd do well in school or volunteer to work for a very visible charity. Sometimes they'd pat me on the head, but most of the time they'd ignore me. Even in their home, at their dinner table, I was alone. Lonely. I don't want to go back to that."

He wouldn't either. No matter how much he stayed away, he knew the second he came home, his family would smother him with love.

Familiar sadness for her filled him, but he stopped it from totally taking over. She'd figured all this out on her own, clearly come to terms with it. She was a strong woman. A unique, wonderful person. No one needed to pity her. He might wish he could help her, but he would never, ever feel sorry for her.

The band took a break, and Ricky and Eloise walked back to the table. Tucker and Olivia leaned in together, as if they were telling secrets. But Olivia's face was pinched and Tucker's brow had furrowed.

Ricky tensed.

Eloise walked over and stooped beside Olivia's chair. "Wanna tell me what's going on here?"

Close enough to hear and not wanting to look overly interested in case it was a lover's quarrel, Ricky took his seat.

Tucker said, "We think Olivia might be in labor."

Eloise gasped. "And she flew? You let her get on an airplane this close to her due date?"

"She's not due for another month. Her doctor said it was fine."

Olivia panted out a breath. "Seriously. I'm not due for a month. This might not be labor. Everybody said it was fine for me to fly."

Eloise sighed. "It might have been fine for you to fly, but you're not fine now." She reached across the table, grabbed her small handbag, retrieved her phone and dialed 911. "This is Eloise Vaughn. I'm at the Ritz with a woman who is in labor."

Olivia said, "Really Eloise, that's not necessary.... Oh my God!"

Tucker stiffened. "What?"

Olivia caught Eloise's hand. "Tell them to hurry."

When Eloise finished the call, Olivia squeezed her fingers. "If it's possible, I want to get down to the lobby."

Eloise gaped at her. "The lobby?"

"I don't want to make a scene. Get me downstairs, hide

me somewhere. I don't want anybody to see if my water breaks or hear me if I scream."

There wasn't a woman in the world who wouldn't understand that and Eloise couldn't refuse. "Can you walk?"

Olivia nodded.

She motioned for Ricky to come over to them. "Tucker's going to help Olivia to the door. You and I are going to walk behind them just in case."

Ricky nodded, but memory after memory of Blake's birth tumbled through him. He hadn't been in love with Blake's mother. Basically, they'd been nightclub friends who'd slept together, and she ended up pregnant. He hadn't gone to birthing classes, didn't really want to be in the delivery room—and he hadn't been—but he'd gone to the hospital when Blake was born. The same hospital where his son had ultimately died. And that was probably the same hospital Tucker would direct Olivia to, if only because, like Ricky, he was on their board of directors.

Eloise caught his arm and pulled him in step behind Tucker and Olivia. "Get with the program, slick."

He shook himself out of his reverie. If this were anybody but Tucker and Olivia, the torrent of memories assaulting him right now would have frozen him solid.

But when Olivia's steps faltered, he was right behind her, ready to catch her.

Ricky's limo pulled onto the emergency entrance ramp behind the ambulance with Olivia and Tucker inside. Eloise leaped out the second the car stopped.

She was at the door of the ambulance as they pulled the gurney off and Tucker jumped down.

The pair, Olivia's best friend and her husband, hustled with Olivia into the emergency room.

Ricky held back. Everything inside him told him to leave. Too many bad memories were associated with this hospital. Yet he couldn't seem to get his mouth to form the words to tell Norman to go. His best friend's baby was coming early. Olivia's life could be in jeopardy.

And Eloise was upset. She might have taken control, but he'd felt her vibrating with fear through the entire drive over. He could not leave her.

He slid out of the limo, leaned inside his still open back door and sent Norman home. Blake had taken nineteen hours to make his appearance. Tucker and Olivia's child could take as long or longer.

He ambled into the emergency room, gave his name at the desk and flashed his ID as a member of the board. "I want to be apprised of Olivia Engle's condition every step of the way."

The receptionist shook her head. "I'm sorry, sir. But our privacy policy prevents that unless you're family." She gave him a hopeful look, clearly not wanting to get into a battle of wills with a hospital director.

Tucking his key card into his jacket pocket, he put her out of her misery. "Check with Mr. Engle. He'll tell you it's okay."

She walked away, and, a few minutes later, she returned and told him that Olivia had been taken upstairs to the maternity ward.

Haunted, afraid to go back to the part of the hospital that had the good memories, memories of Blake being born, of holding his son for the first time, of wrapping the tiny, squiggly bundle in a blanket before securing him in his car seat, Ricky took his time walking to the elevator and then down the long cool corridor to the waiting room of the maternity ward.

An hour went by. He sat. He paced. He sat some more, elbows on his knees, hands dropped between his legs. Eventually, he stood, untied his tie, undid the first two buttons of his shirt and walked to the intensive care unit in the children's ward, where he stood by the window and stared at the empty cribs.

If he closed his eyes, he could see his son bandaged and bruised, an IV locked into his hand, his little chest barely rising and falling as a ventilator did his breathing for him.

Tears filled his eyes, reviving his shame. Then he realized Tucker's baby might be too small, too weak, and the newest member of the happy Engle family might spend his or her first days or weeks or even a year in the same crib as Blake.

His shame morphed into fear. Real fear that Tucker and Olivia might face the devastation of losing a child. He could feel every bit of sorrow that would overwhelm them and cursed. That shouldn't happen to anyone. But Olivia and Tucker? They were special. They didn't deserve this.

The rustle of skirts interrupted the quiet, and he turned to see Eloise walking down the hall.

"Hey."

"Hey." He frowned. "This is a private ward. How'd you get in here?"

She showed him a key card. "Tucker gave me this and said to find you. How did *you* get in here?"

He pulled the key card just like Tucker's from his tuxedo jacket pocket.

"Wow. You two must be some big-time donors."

"We're on the board." He sucked in a breath. "How's Olivia?"

She winced. "Not in labor. The doctor's keeping her overnight just to be sure, but she's fine."

He breathed a sigh of relief, so glad Tucker and Olivia's baby would be okay that for several seconds he couldn't function. Finally, he ran his hand across the back of his neck and forced his muscles and brain to relax. "That's good."

She looked around. "It's so quiet here."

"That's normal in the children's ICU."

He expected a question or two. She'd earned the right

to ask them. He felt her curiosity like a living, breathing thing. Still, she said nothing.

His respect for her grew. He'd told her he didn't want her to know his past, his pain, because he didn't want her to treat him any differently—or, worse, to pity him. And if the casual way she behaved around him was anything to go by, she hadn't looked him up on the internet and hadn't asked his friends for information.

It boggled his mind that she hadn't investigated him. If the tables were turned, he would have been driven crazy until he gave in to his curiosity, but he would have given in. She'd been a rock. She was probably the most trustworthy person on the planet.

"Good evening, Mr. Langley." Regina walked up to them, giving Eloise a quick once-over. "And who is this?"

He looked from Regina to Eloise, who met his gaze with as much curiosity about how he'd answer as Regina had.

Their gazes locked. She'd gone to all his parties with him, always kept up the charade and always looked pretty for him, even though it probably meant working like a Christmas elf to get that party's dress altered. He'd refused to tell her his secrets and she'd accepted it.

He couldn't think of her as nothing but a fake date anymore. He might not be her real boyfriend, but she was more than a partner in a charade.

He caught her hand and squeezed it. "She's a friend."

Eloise smiled.

Regina said, "Well, it's quiet up here tonight. Stay as long as you like."

It didn't seem right to stand with Eloise at the window to the room where his son had died. He didn't want her to see his grief. Plus, with Olivia fine and the baby out of danger, there was no reason to stay.

"Actually, we were just on our way out."

"Good night then."

"Good night, Regina." He directed Eloise to the elevator. "I sent Norman home. We're going to have to get a taxi."

"A taxi! Do you know how expensive taxis are?"

He laughed, then realized that's exactly what she'd intended for him to do. But the sights and the sounds of the hospital kept him grounded in reality, and he suddenly felt guilty for those three seconds of happiness.

No matter how much Eloise lifted his spirits, in his heart he knew he didn't deserve to be whole.

CHAPTER EIGHT

ELOISE ROLLED OVER in bed the next morning, not able to get herself to crawl out and face the day.

She wasn't the kind to overthink things, but why would someone choose to wait in the intensive care unit of the children's ward instead of the maternity waiting room?

She let the obvious reasons flit through her brain. Maybe Ricky had spent time there himself as a child. Or maybe one of his siblings had. Or maybe he'd had a child who'd been there. Maybe a child born prematurely, as Tucker and Olivia's child had almost been the night before.

The last one made so much sense that new scenarios began rolling through her head. Scary scenarios. Things his friends' wives would call a tragedy. Things she had no basis to believe. Things that had no grounding in reality.

With a growl, she shoved off the covers, climbed out of bed and shuffled to the kitchen. Laura Beth already sat at the little round table, drinking tea.

"Hey."

"Hey. You're up early for someone who was at a party last night."

She walked to the counter and started making a pot of coffee. "We took Olivia to the hospital."

Laura Beth gasped. "Last night? Is she okay?"

"False labor. She's fine. Baby's fine."

"But…"

She faced Laura Beth. "But what?"

"There's but in your voice. Like there's a catch. She's fine but she's on bed rest or something. What's the catch?"

"There is none. It was just false labor. She's really fine." She bit her lower lip. "But my fake date did something that puzzled me."

"What?"

"He waited in the children's ICU instead of the maternity waiting room."

"Maybe he thought something would be wrong with the baby, so he waited there."

She gasped and closed her eyes. *Of course. That made so much more sense.* His choice of waiting place wasn't about him but Olivia's baby.

Unfortunately, by the time she walked to the table and sat, she'd poked a hole in that theory. "Isn't there a neonatal ICU? One just for newborns?"

Laura Beth shrugged. "I don't know. I don't know much about hospitals, but there may be a special ICU for newborns."

Confused again, Eloise sucked in a breath. "Well, he's also on the hospital board, so maybe he was just looking around, checking on things." She thought of the nurse who'd talked to him and grimaced. "No. That's not it either. A nurse came up to him. She acted as if she knows him."

"If he's on the board, of course she knows him."

She shook her head. "No. This was more like she knew him personally."

Laura Beth winced. "Was she young and pretty?"

"Middle-aged but very pretty. Still, it wasn't that. The way she reacted to him was more like she was accustomed to seeing him." She tried to remember their conversation. "She said stay as long as you like…as if he'd been in the ward before, staring into that ICU room."

Picking up her empty cup, Laura Beth rose from the table. "I think you're making more out of this than you should because you're trying to figure out the 'tragedy' those dinner party wives told you about." She shook her head. "Think it through. His friend's wife was in the hospital, maybe in early labor. That about stopped *my* heart. So I'm sure it scared him too. He might have simply gone to the children's ICU not remembering there'd be a NICU."

She frowned. "Maybe." Her brain could accept that, but her heart disagreed. There was something about the way he stood in front of that window, staring inside.

Her disappointment rattled through her. He'd called her his friend the night before. Yet, here she sat, trying to guess what had happened in his life because he didn't trust her enough to tell her.

"Bruce is taking me skating at Rockefeller Center today."

Not wanting to be thought of as that sad girl anymore, Eloise pasted a smile on her face for her roommate. "Cool."

"I might need to borrow that big navy blue parka of yours."

"Sure."

"You won't be using it?"

"No." She sighed. "We're going to another formal party tonight."

Laura Beth laughed. "Hey, I'd kill to go to even one of those parties. You've been to six or seven."

"Bruce hasn't asked you to one?"

Laura Beth's face reddened and she busied herself with tidying the area around the sink. "No."

Realizing her mistake, Eloise quickly said, "Well, be glad. They sort of get boring after a while. Repetitive." Plus, when they danced, she wanted to melt in Ricky's arms, but he held her two feet away.

She wouldn't tell Laura Beth that, though. She wouldn't be a "sad girl" with the puppy dog eyes anymore. "Usually, I'd spend the weekends before Christmas window shopping." With her subway pass, she could get anywhere in the city and see all the decorations. But what she liked best was Central Park. She'd go there to watch the white horses pulling gilded carriages and dream about someday taking a carriage ride. But that was another one of those silly things she didn't confide to her friends.

"This year, I'm so busy with Ricky and parties and making new gowns out of old ones that I haven't done any of the things I like to do."

And, today, the need to do something normal, to be herself, swelled in her like a tidal wave. She was losing herself in a man who didn't want her. When he was gone, and he would be, she'd be even more alone than she felt now.

Laura Beth shook her head. "Everybody in New York can do what you want to do. This year you get to go to parties. Enjoy it."

As Laura Beth left the room, Eloise squeezed her eyes shut as the truth bombarded her. The tidal wave that filled her with longing wasn't to do something normal alone. It was to do something normal with Ricky. To go window shopping with him. To go on that carriage ride with him. To see the tree at Rockefeller Center with him. She wanted to do something normal *with him* because she wanted him to be normal with her. At the big formal balls, he could dodge her questions. Hell, he could dodge actually spending time with her just by talking to his friends or dancing.

And she was tired of having dinner with people she didn't really know. Tired of not being allowed to let herself go when they danced. Tired of pretending to be happy.

But, most of all, she was tired of pretending it was okay that the whole world knew his past, his secrets, but she couldn't know because he didn't want it to affect how she treated him.

Didn't he know her well enough yet to understand that she'd always treat him with respect?

Why didn't he trust her?

That night when he arrived to pick her up, the insult

of being the only one in his social circle who didn't know his tragedy stiffened her muscles and put an icy tone in her voice.

He slid her cape on her shoulders, covering her silver dress. "You look great."

She faced him and smiled, but her cheeks rebelled at the attempt to lift her mouth, and her smile was barely a curve of her lips. "Thank you."

He opened the door. She led him into the hall and to the stairway. She said nothing as they walked down the steps, through the lobby and to the car. But she couldn't very well walk past Norman without a greeting.

"Good evening, Norman."

He touched the rim of his hat. "Evening, ma'am."

She slid into the car. Ricky slid in behind her. Neither said a word.

He cleared his throat. "So…difficult day today?"

She continued to look out the window. "No. It was a normal day. A little house cleaning. A little sewing."

"That's right. You work on your clothes the day of a party."

"Yes."

"Well, that silver thing you're wearing is really pretty."

She wanted to tell him that she'd struggled not to make it a dress with a low back. She loved that style. But in the end, she'd decided to give it a full back for him. She knew he didn't like having to touch her so much.

Her nerve endings caught fire. Two parties ago, he'd held her hand and brought her close, like somebody who liked her. They'd drunk tequila like silly friends, and he'd almost kissed her. Now they were back to being polite strangers.

Every time they took one step forward, he took two steps back. Tonight it cut through her like a knife, shredding her heart, bruising her soul. Even if he didn't want to love her, he should like her. She'd been nothing but nice to him.

The car stopped at another posh condo building. She faced him. "This is a private residence?"

"Yes. Binnie and Dennis are hosting a small gathering."

"I'm in a *gown*."

He looked at her. His big, beautiful brown eyes were totally clueless.

She threw her hands in the air. "I am not going to a private party in a gown!" Tears pushed behind her eyelids and threatened to show themselves. She'd been so upset with him all day that this little incident was toppling her over the edge. The last thing she wanted was for him to see it.

She glanced around. "Look, just go alone. You'll be fine. And I'll be fine. I can get myself home. I'm not sure where the subway is, but I can find it."

Before either Norman or Ricky could react, she shoved open her car door and jumped out.

He scrambled out after her. "Whoa! Whoa! Wait!"

"Forget it."

The whole situation closed in on her. Smiling for people she didn't know. Spending time with a guy who clearly didn't like her back. And missed opportunities. Obvious times he could have kissed her or been kind to her that he'd backed away from. She'd poured her heart out to him, not just because the conversation lent itself to her being honest, but because she wanted him to know her.

But he didn't want her to know him, and he certainly didn't want to know her. He'd listened to her story with bare minimum curiosity, and when she was done talking he hadn't consoled her. Leaving her empty. Feeling like no one. Nothing.

Who'd have thought going out with someone could make her so lonely?

Her arm suddenly jerked back and she was spun around.

"I made a mistake by not calling today to tell you what to wear. I'm sorry. We'll go home. You can change."

Her ridiculous tears spilled over. "It's too late now. By

the time we'd get back, they'd be halfway through dinner." She swiped at her tears. "Just go. Go see your friends. Have fun."

He tugged her arm to bring her closer. "At least let Norman take you home."

Fresh tears flooded her eyes. Somewhere deep inside her, she'd hoped *he'd* take her home. Ignore what she said about going to the party without her and comfort her instead.

But that was stupid. He didn't like her. He didn't want to like her. She was a hired date. It was okay to be upset that she was in the wrong outfit, but she couldn't be upset that he wasn't giving something that wasn't part of their deal.

Once again, she probably looked insane to him.

They walked to the car in silence, across the shiny rain-wet pavement. White Christmas lights adorned the trees lining the exclusive street. Huge evergreen wreaths with red and green plaid ribbons and shiny red Christmas balls decorated the double-door front entrance of Binnie and Dennis's building.

When they reached the car, Ricky opened the door for her. She slid inside and he closed the door behind her.

The sound was so final that her heart beat out a fearful tattoo. What had she done? By not going to this dinner party with him, she was proving he didn't need her anymore. He could go alone.

She groaned. She needed the job going out with him could provide. She needed his connections. And now she was throwing it all away because she'd worn the wrong dress?

She leaned back on the seat. That wasn't it. His not telling her about the party was a symptom of the bigger thing he wouldn't tell her. His tragedy.

He'd called her a friend.

But he didn't share his secrets.

And she liked him.

But most days he was only nice to her because he had to be. And he hadn't cared when she'd told him her secrets.

Yet she liked him.

A lot.

Felt some kind of soul connection that he obviously didn't feel.

That was the real humiliation. Longing for something that he didn't see.

The limo door suddenly opened. Ricky slid inside.

She sat up. "What are you doing?"

"I'm taking you home. I called Binnie and explained you weren't feeling well and bowed out."

"What?"

"I bowed out." He studied her face. "I can see something's really wrong."

And he cared?

She sniffed. Hope tried to nudge in, but she reminded herself of the truth and quashed it. If he didn't care that her husband had died and her parents had disowned her, he certainly wouldn't want to know that she felt left out, rejected, because he wouldn't confide in her. And she absolutely wouldn't tell him that she was falling for him. That would be the ultimate humiliation.

Wiping her eyes, she stuck with the convenient. "It's pretty bad to be the only woman in a gown at a dinner party. It would make me look stupid...clueless about social conventions."

He winced. "Sorry about that."

"It's fine."

Norman started the car and pulled out into the street.

Ricky settled back on the seat. "It feels weird to be going home."

It didn't to her. The sooner she got away from him, the sooner she could cry, call herself every kind of fool and splurge by drinking one of the precious cups of hot cocoa she'd squirreled away for nights like this.

"I mean, I'm dressed and you're dressed." He turned and caught her gaze. He smiled slightly. "Seems like a waste."

"I can wear this dress tomorrow." She glanced out the window, then faced him again. The crying might have been her fault. Might have been an overreaction. Might have made her look even more foolish than she already did to him. But forgetting to tell her how to dress? That was his fault. "Unless we're going to a dinner party tomorrow."

"I'll check the invitation when I get home and call you."

"I'd appreciate that."

He cleared his throat. "I still don't think we should just go home."

"The deal was twelve parties."

"I know. But missing one is sort of reneging on the deal." He glanced at her. "If you enjoy them."

She picked at her cape. "Sometimes I do." When he was himself. A normal guy. Which, lately, wasn't often.

"At least let me buy you dinner."

"I'm not hungry."

But even as she said the words her stomach growled.

"I think you are hungry."

"Stop feeling sorry for me!" The shout was out before she could stop it. "For Pete's sake! You hate people feeling sorry for you, so you should damn well understand I hate people feeling sorry for me!"

He grimaced. "Got it."

Shame filled her again. She didn't know why she was so emotional tonight, but she was. And she needed to get away from him.

She turned to the window and looked out at the city decorated for the holidays, the festive lights that seemed to be mocking her.

"So if you could go anywhere you wanted to tonight, where would it be?"

She squeezed her eyes shut. "You're not going to drop this, are you?"

"I always try to make up for my mistakes."

So now she was a mistake? "Terrific."

"Where would you want to go…if you could go anywhere you wanted?"

She was halfway tempted to tell him Paris just to shut him up. But what if he actually took her there? She wasn't risking that. Imagine how much she could embarrass herself across the pond? No, thanks. Enough New Yorkers thought she was a sad girl with puppy dog eyes. She didn't need to add Europeans to the list.

She scoured her brain for somewhere reasonable to tell him but somewhere he'd nonetheless refuse.

When it came to her, she smiled.

"What I'd really like is a carriage ride in Central Park."

He sniffed. "It's raining."

"I know. Drat. Stupid suggestion." She sighed. "Might as well just go home."

He pulled out his cell phone. "Now, hold on. Let's not get ahead of ourselves." He hit a button. "David? Can you do me a favor and arrange a carriage ride?" He paused, then laughed. "Right now, actually." He paused again, waiting a minute or two before he said, "South entrance? Great. Thanks."

"So it looks like we have a carriage."

She gaped at him. "It's raining!"

"It's also what you want."

She sighed. The one time she really and truly didn't want him to be nice to her, when she wanted him to be his usual self-absorbed self so she could just go home and wallow in her own misery, he decided to be nice.

"I want the carriage ride on a sunny day or a warm night." Now she sounded like a spoiled child. "Not a night when it's raining."

"We got a carriage with a roof. And they have blankets."

He seemed so happily proud of himself that she had to fight not to roll her eyes. She wouldn't talk him out of this, and she had always wanted to go for a carriage ride through Central Park. Might as well just enjoy it. She'd have plenty of time to wallow in misery on Christmas day.

"Thank you."

"You're welcome." He tapped the window to give Norman instructions. In ten minutes, the limo stopped.

The entire street sparkled with raindrops. Although there were no stars, the moon hung overhead, a bright round ball. White clouds rolled by, sometimes hiding it, but eventually it would appear again, as if smiling at her, telling her to relax, everything would be okay.

After a short chat with Norman, Ricky helped her onto the red seat of a white carriage, sat beside her and tucked the covers around her.

"You're going to be cold in that cape."

"I don't care." And suddenly she didn't. She'd wanted one of these rides since she was a little girl. She would listen to the moon and not miss a minute of it.

As the horse-driven carriage clomped its way into Central Park, she huddled tightly under the blanket.

"So of all the places to go, things to do, why this?"

"Once when we drove past as kids, I almost had my dad talked into a ride. But my mother vetoed it at the last minute."

"Oh. Sorry about that."

"Not your fault." She laughed. The brisk air filled her lungs. The shiny wet path sparkled like the road to a fairy-tale castle. "Besides, I'm here now." She cuddled into the covers, leaned back and took a long drink of the fresh air again.

He pulled a bit of the blanket onto his lap. It wasn't cold enough to snow, but it was wet, the kind of damp cold that seeped into bones. She didn't blame him for wanting to cover up.

"I've never done this either."

She peeked at him. The steady clip-clop of the horse's hooves filled the dark, wet air. "Really?"

"Though I did bring my son here…to Central Park."

Ricky's tongue tripped over the awkward words. He shouldn't have mentioned Blake. All that did was open floodgates for questions. But tonight's mistake had been big enough that she'd cried. She'd tried to hide it or stop it, but she'd lost the battle and he'd lost all control. He'd have given her every cent of his fortune to get her to stop.

A carriage ride was a small price to pay.

Before she could ask questions that would lead to answers he wasn't ready to give, he added, "Blake loved it. It was summer." He huddled more deeply under the blanket, bringing them closer together as they passed bare trees, shiny with cold rain that might turn to ice. "I took him to the carousel, but there are a bunch of baseball fields near there, and he went nuts when he saw them." He laughed and shook his head. "It's hard to tell an eighteen-month-old that he can't play with the big kids."

Her gaze stayed on his face, her expression curious but tempered. She'd wanted to know about his circumstances and he'd refused to tell her. She would recognize this was a huge concession.

He cleared his throat. "Anyway, I'd thought about taking him on a carriage ride, but, luckily, he got tired and we went home."

"You have a son?"

He shrugged, not able to tell her Blake had died, if only because he knew he couldn't handle the pain remembering his son's death would bring.

But he also felt oddly free that he'd spoken about his little boy. Because everyone was so silent about him, sometimes it felt as if he'd never existed. "Yeah."

She caught his gaze, examined his face and said, "You and his mother aren't together?"

He shook his head. "No. We were essentially strangers

who created a child." He winced. "We sound like terrible people. We weren't."

She put her hand on his sleeve. "I get it. No need to explain."

He suddenly wished with all his heart that he could explain, that he could talk about his son, his *baby*. He longed to reminisce about good times. To remember his little boy fondly. To laugh.

But all those things did was remind him that, in the end, he hadn't had what it took to be a father.

He shook that off. He'd have plenty of time for guilt on Christmas morning. "So, anyway, she's part of the reason the search engine I created is so thorough. The system was already in beta testing when she told she was pregnant. Her pregnancy caused me to add a few more rules to an already elaborate algorithm."

Confusion flitted through her blue eyes. "Why?"

He shrugged. "She was a single woman living alone in an expensive condo in New York City."

"She must have had a great job."

"She had no job."

"Rich parents?"

"Nope."

"Oh."

"Exactly. She'd gotten the condo from the last guy she dated. After she told me she was pregnant, I ended up picking up the tab for her utilities, groceries…all her monthly expenses."

"Yikes."

"Not that I minded, but I knew I had been bamboozled." Needing to change the subject quickly, before she started asking questions, he said, "What about you? Any bad dates in your history?"

She cuddled closer, wrapped her hands around his arm and closed her eyes. Their breaths misted on the chilled air.

He knew she'd nestled into him for warmth, but his chest loosened. His nerves settled. She wasn't upset anymore.

"In high school, I only dated boys my parents approved of. In college…" She shrugged. "You know that story."

"Yeah."

They lapsed into comfortable silence. The horse's hooves clip-clopped. The freezing night air bought them closer under the blanket. Everything inside him stilled. For the first time in eighteen months, he was calm. Totally calm.

After a few minutes, he realized she'd fallen asleep. Her crying must have worn her out. He tucked the covers more tightly around her and leaned back, closing his eyes and enjoying the fact that he wasn't working or thinking about work or at a party talking about work.

After a while, the driver turned the carriage around and headed back. The air became colder and colder and they nestled tighter and tighter under the blanket, sharing their warmth.

A contented smile framed Eloise's beautiful face. He studied her perfect complexion, her small nose, the fan of black eyelashes that rested on her pale skin. He'd never met a woman so physically perfect. A princess.

His brow furrowed. An abandoned princess. Somebody nobody wanted.

When the carriage stopped, he shook her gently. "Time to get up."

Her eyes popped open. "I fell asleep?"

He laughed. "Only for a little while." The longing to kiss her bubbled up again. If anyone deserved love, it was her. Their gazes locked. A spray of rain tumbled from the branch of a nearby tree and drummed against the carriage roof. Seconds ticked off the clock, as they gazed into each other's eyes and desire warred with common sense. He had nothing to offer her but money…and himself. A broken, guilt-ridden man, who might end up hurting her more than her parents had.

The driver appeared at the side of the carriage, breaking the mood and taking the decision to kiss her out of his hands.

"Ride's been paid for, including tip." He grinned. "For which I add a hearty thank-zyou."

Not wanting Eloise to know he'd paid double for the ride to assure a happy driver, Ricky shoved the covers away. "Come on."

He helped her down from the carriage and directed her across the street to the waiting limo.

Norman pushed off the front bumper and opened the door as Ricky and Eloise approached.

"Nice ride?" he asked Eloise as she got closer to the car. She smiled. "Very nice."

Ricky got into the limo behind her. With the heater blasting, they had no need to huddle together. And he missed it. Settling onto the supple leather seat a few feet away from her, he missed her warmth. He missed comforting her. Nothing made him feel normal the way pleasing her had. But there was more to it than that. He always felt a connection, a yearning when he was with her that went beyond simple bonding. It was like they belonged together.

But he knew in his heart that had to be wrong. He didn't belong with anybody. Not only was he so broken he didn't have anything to give, but he hurt the people who got closest to him and he absolutely refused to hurt Eloise.

In front of her apartment door, she smiled slightly. "Thank you. I had a great time."

"You feel better then?"

"Yes, though I'm sorry I got all hysterical."

"Believe it or not, I'm not." He paused. "It was nice to do something out of the ordinary. To talk about things other than work."

Her hopeful gaze met his. "You should do it more often."

He glanced away. "Maybe."

"Well, it was fun and I appreciate it."

He caught her gaze again. Saw the smile in her eyes. Felt the ice around his heart melt.

A need to be worthy of her raced through him, heating his blood. A wish that he could love her rose from the very bottom of his broken, battered soul. His whole body vibrated with the desire to be whole. To be ready. To be everything she needed him to be.

She reached out and wrapped her arms around his waist, hugging him to her.

He knew she meant it as a thanks, but sensation after sensation rippled through him. Trust. Need. Yearning. They were so strong he couldn't resist the urge to raise his arms and settle them around her shoulders. When her arms tightened in response, his arms tightened too.

He closed his eyes, fighting the longing to kiss her that swelled in him. He reminded himself he was broken. Told himself she deserved better. But the carriage ride, the look of contentment on her face, the way she had listened to him without asking unwanted questions, without judgment, all formed like bright pictures in his head, blocking out the negative, until he couldn't fight instinct anymore. He opened his eyes, bent down and put his lips on hers.

At first he didn't think she would respond, but her lips came alive slowly, tentatively, as if she were every bit as afraid of their feelings for each other as he was.

Something dark and possessive rose up in him. He deepened the kiss, and she followed, again slowly, again tentatively. Their tongues twined, and his heart overflowed with something so intense it took his breath away.

This was right. He knew it was right.

When he could stop thinking about Blake, about his mistakes, about his stupidity, all he felt was rightness with her. A click.

But even that scared him. When he was with her, nothing else in the world mattered. But maybe that was the scariest thing of all. Could he love someone so much that he'd forget his son? Was it even right to love someone so much that he forgot his son? His baby. His heart.

He pulled back, knowing every bit of his turmoil, every bit of his need was in his eyes.

She smiled tentatively. "Good night."

"Good night."

He tried to turn away, but his feet felt rooted to the spot. Her warmth drew him. He wanted to stay close to it. But he also didn't want to hurt her.

He started down the hall before he lost his conviction. The aftereffects of the kiss hummed through him. Part pleasure, part yearning, they drove him to race down the steps without faltering.

As good as this felt right now, he knew getting involved with her—with anyone—could be the biggest mistake of his life.

Or hers.

CHAPTER NINE

ELOISE STEPPED INTO her apartment, closed the door and leaned against it.

He kissed me.

They hadn't just had a private evening in the carriage ride she'd longed for since childhood, but he'd kissed her. Not forced by mistletoe. Not a little tipsy from tequila. But with real emotion.

She walked into the cold, silent apartment, wishing Laura Beth wasn't dating Tucker's vice president. The late-night coffeehouse meeting hadn't turned into a job for Laura Beth. It had become a romance. And now Ricky had kissed her and she just wanted to share the news, but there was no one to share it with.

The sound of the key in the lock of their apartment door clicked into the silent room. She spun around to see Laura Beth and Bruce stumbling into the apartment.

When they saw her, they both froze. "Eloise? What are you doing here?"

She smiled, hoping her entire face wasn't glowing with joy. "I live here."

Laura Beth gave a fake laugh. "Right. I just thought your party would last longer." She faced her boyfriend. "You remember Bruce?"

She stepped forward and shook his hand. "We weren't actually introduced."

He smiled politely. "It's a pleasure to meet you."

The air tingled with awkwardness. She normally didn't dislike someone on sight, but Bruce's slick good looks gave her an odd feeling. His blond hair was too yellow. His tanning booth tan too dark. It was as if he was trying to look like a surfer king. But he didn't live in the tropics. He lived in bitter cold New York City, where it rained when it should be snowing and snowed when it was least convenient.

His gaze slid to Laura Beth's and he nudged his head in the direction of the bedrooms.

Eloise's skin actually felt like little bugs were crawling on it.

Laura Beth pointed down the hall. "I'm just going to get some things from my room, then Bruce and I will be off again."

"Okay."

Laura Beth scooted away.

She found herself alone with Bruce, who looked her up and down, as if he were judging her or comparing her to Laura Beth...or just being plain sleazy.

She thought of the mother of Ricky's son. A woman who'd taken a condo from her first boyfriend and used her pregnancy to get living expenses from Ricky. And suddenly everything Ricky had done in the past weeks, his hesitancy, his fears, made perfect sense.

Laura Beth raced into the living area again. With a small overnight bag in her hands, she grinned at Eloise. "I'll see you in the morning."

Eloise nodded and the pair left.

Considering sleazy Bruce, and perhaps making incorrect comparisons to Ricky's child's mother, she walked down the hall to her bedroom, understanding why Ricky was taking his time with this romance. Not everybody in this world was trustworthy. He'd been burned. Obviously badly. He would not want to be burned again. That's why it took him so long to trust her.

Some of her joy returned. Ricky was a good, honest guy.

And he liked her. If that kiss was anything to go by, he *really* liked her.

Plus, she'd rushed into things with Wayne.

If anybody understood the reasoning behind taking things slowly and valuing every step, it should be her.

So if she understood, why did thinking about Bruce suddenly make her feel trouble was on the horizon?

Barefoot and wearing only a fleece robe, Ricky trudged to his silent kitchen the next morning. At the counter, he pressed the button to reveal his coffeemaker. He pulled a single-serve container from the fancy holder, tossed it inside and set his coffee to brewing, remembering how Eloise still missed her stolen coffeemaker.

He laughed, then squeezed his eyes shut. Something about her always made him laugh. Made him forget. Made him feel normal.

Dear God he liked her. But in the light of day, he wasn't sure starting a real relationship was a good idea. He had more dark days than light. True, being with her helped him forget Blake, but he wasn't sure that was appropriate. And he did not want to hurt her.

Yet it seemed so right.

Determined not to think about it and to let nature take its course, he reached for the week's accumulated mail and rifled through it. A shiny brochure slid through his fingers. The hospital's annual Christmas plea.

He pulled it out, curious not just because he was a director, but also because he wanted the hospital to get donations. A collage of pictures of the kids who'd been through the hospital for various reasons populated the cover page. He liked it. Simple but effective, it told the story of how the hospital saved lives. Many lives. Especially the lives of children.

But when he saw the picture of Blake, a tiny photo tucked among all the others, his heart stopped.

What the hell?

Not only had they not gotten permission to use that photograph, but who would have been stupid enough to think he'd want his deceased son's picture on a brochure?

He grabbed his cell phone, hit speed dial for his assistant and waited two rings before David answered.

"Who authorized Blake's picture to be in the collage on the front of the hospital brochure?"

"Blake's picture is in that collage?" Horror rippled through David's voice. "That has to be a mistake."

"Call hospital PR. Have the remaining brochures destroyed. And find out who gave them permission to use that picture."

"Absolutely."

Conversation ended, Ricky grabbed the brochure and tore it to shreds. Of all the damned stupid mistakes!

He raked his fingers through his hair and reached for his phone again, only to realize he was about to call Eloise.

Eloise.

Why did he automatically want to call her? What would he say? That his son was dead? That some idiot screwed up and put Blake's picture on a million brochures? That his heart was broken? That everything he'd felt while watching his son struggle for life had come storming back in living color?

He squeezed his eyes shut as misery reminded him this was his life. *This* was what he had to offer Eloise. Sharp shards of pain that pierced his heart at unexpected moments of memory. Deep depressions that dragged him down so far he couldn't speak some days.

How foolish was it to believe she would want this? How selfish was it?

He sucked in a breath, tossed the phone to the counter, grabbed his coffee and strode to his office.

He considered calling her to tell her they wouldn't be seeing each other anymore. No matter how much hurt he heard in her voice, he would endure it, simply because he knew a little sting now saved her real pain later. But he hadn't fulfilled his end of their deal. He couldn't stop seeing her until he found her a job.

His resolve sharpened. He had to protect her. That meant he had to get her a job. Then he could tell her he'd changed his mind about going to the rest of his parties and wish her well with her future employer, and she would be out of his life.

When Ricky's knock sounded on her door that night, Eloise drew in a deep breath. The night before he'd talked about his personal life, his son, and he'd kissed her. He liked her. No matter what feelings creepy Bruce instilled, she knew Ricky liked her. She wasn't going to screw this up by being afraid or overeager. He needed time to trust her, and she would give him time. After all, they still had plenty of parties to attend, and she'd be dancing with a man who had kissed her like a guy falling. These next few weeks might be the happiest of her life.

Her heart shivered with anticipation. She drew another breath, subdued the bright smile that might scare him silly, and opened the door.

"Hey."

"Hey."

If the dull expression in his dark eyes wasn't clue enough, his slow entry into her apartment told her he regretted kissing her. The urge to squeeze her eyes shut surged, but she stopped it, reminding herself he had a child with a woman who wasn't exactly scrupulous. He hadn't said much beyond the fact that he supported her at one time, but what if they'd had a disagreement and she'd taken his child away from him? What if she hadn't just moved to another city or state? What if she'd disappeared? What if the tragedy in his life was that he had a little boy he adored but he couldn't see him or be part of his life?

She hadn't seen any sign that a child had ever been in his apartment. No one at any of the parties ever asked him about his child, proving that was his sore spot. What worse could an unscrupulous mother do than take away a beloved child from a doting father?

If Eloise wanted him to open up to her, she had to prove herself to be trustworthy. She couldn't overreact when he pulled back. She should respect it and show him he could trust her not to probe but to let him come around in his own time.

"You look very nice."

He glanced down at his tux and black topcoat. "I look the same as I always do."

She laughed. "I know. You wear it well."

He sniffed a sound that was almost a chuckle—almost.

Her heart picked up a bit. Rome was not built in a day. Neither was trust.

She handed him her cape. He slid it on her shoulders. "You look nice tonight. But you always look nice, too."

"Thanks." The soft pink dress she'd altered hadn't been much of a task. The quietly elegant strapless gown hugged every curve and accented her pale skin, but it wasn't fancy. She'd deliberately not gone flashy or fancy, but stuck with her own taste rather than fashion. Up to now, she'd worked to make herself look like the perfect sparkly date for a rich guy. Tonight, she wanted to be herself, to give him a taste of the real her.

Which, now that she added it to everything else, was probably the smart thing to do. From here on out, she wasn't Eloise Vaughn, fake date. She was the real Eloise Vaughn, the woman she wanted Ricky Langley to fall in love with.

He opened the door and she walked out. "So how was your day?"

He wouldn't meet her gaze. "My day was very long."

"How so?"

"Special project."

She stopped at the top of the steps, not really wanting to push, but seeing this as an opportunity they could connect as real people. "Yeah? Anything you can talk about?"

"I'd prefer not to, but suffice to say I'm having trouble figuring out an angle for a problem I have to solve as soon as possible."

"You're sure it's nothing I can help you with?"

He hesitated but eventually said, "Yes."

They walked down the steps and out into the frigid night. "We need snow."

He sniffed again, an acknowledgment of her comment but not quite a reply. Still, she wasn't daunted. The man had kissed her because he'd wanted to. She'd even tried to dissuade him by not kissing him back, but he hadn't stopped. He'd deepened the kiss. He might be afraid to trust, but he was falling. She could feel it. And if she wanted him, then she had to give him time.

As they walked under the portico of the entryway of Santana Lawson's Montauk beach house, an itch formed under Ricky's collar. In her gorgeous pink dress, Eloise looked amazing. Even more amazing than she looked in the fancy, sparkly dresses she typically wore. The feeling of rightness with her had risen at least three times in the limo. He fought them all, not for himself, but to protect her. Still, this would be a long night.

He guided her into the entryway where Santana stood greeting guests. Wearing a black tux, a black shirt and a black tie, with his shoulder-length hair pulled into a tight ponytail at his nape, Santana played the part of unconventional investor to the hilt.

"So, somebody finally got this guy out into the circuit again."

Eloise laughed lightly. "It wasn't so difficult."

Santana kissed her hand. "Not for somebody as beautiful as you, I'm sure."

Jealousy licked in Ricky's stomach like the strike of a match, but he shook it off. He couldn't like her. Didn't have anything to offer her but years of misery. Jealousy had no place in this deal.

Grasping Santana's hand, he said, "Thank you for inviting us."

Santana's eyes sparked with curiosity. Ricky could see he wanted to ask a million questions, but he only said, "It's my pleasure." He pointed down the hall. "Ballroom's the first door on the left."

Eloise's shoes clicked softly on the Italian marble floors. She sucked in a breath to compose herself, the way she always did before they entered a party. At the beginning of their arrangement, she hadn't known most of his friends. She'd had to alter dresses to fit in. Yet, she'd never groused. Never complained. She just did what she had to do.

Admiration for her rattled through him, and he suddenly realized how intensely he would miss her. When he found her a job and they stopped seeing each other, he would sit in his quiet office and think of these nights…and miss her.

She placed her hand in the crook of his elbow. "Ready?"

Their gazes met. He reminded himself that what he felt didn't matter. He had to think about her. Her future. Her happiness.

"Yes. I'm ready."

But the reminders didn't make him feel any better. The sadness that flashed through him wasn't the red-hot searing pain of missing Blake. It was softer. More like remorse than regret.

He walked them to their assigned table and was surprised to find world-renowned clothes designer Bob Barbie was headed there too. He only recognized Bob because the designer had hit a rough patch the year before and Ricky had lent him money.

"I'm not sure how I got to sit with you business geeks," Bob said, laughing as he held out a chair for his date.

"We're glad to have you, Bob," Ricky said, turning to Eloise. "This is Eloise Vaughn." He smiled. "Eloise, this is Bob Barbie."

Her eyes widened. "*The* Bob Barbie?"

Bob smiled as if bored. "Yes."

"Oh my gosh! It's such a pleasure to meet you. I loved your fall collection."

"Everyone did." His eyes narrowed as he studied Eloise. He said, "Humph," then he turned to his date, effectively closing the conversation.

Eloise leaned into Ricky and whispered, "I don't think he liked my dress."

He frowned. His gaze automatically fell to the strapless pink gown. Cleavage peeked at him and he licked his dry lips. Nothing about her was imperfect. Everything was touchable. Tempting. His fingers itched to touch her as his brain tingled with the longing to think about what it could be like for them.

He swallowed, fighting needs that struggled to overcome common sense.

Eloise tapped her fingers on the table. "Pink's not a Christmas color. Maybe he doesn't like people wearing un-holiday colors during the holidays."

He cleared his throat. "Don't be silly."

She laughed. "I guess that is pretty silly."

"All right. I give up." Bob's angry comment rolled across the table. "Who are you wearing?"

"Excuse me?"

"Whose gown? I've run through everybody I know and I can't figure it out. So just tell me."

Eloise laughed. "You can't guess because I made this gown."

Bob's eyes narrowed. "Yourself?"

She winced. "Yes."

"But you bought someone's pattern…"

She shook her head. "No. I made it myself."

He propped his hand on his waist. "You're lying."

Anger stiffened Ricky's spine. "I hope you didn't just call my date a liar, Bob."

He waved a hand. "I'm just saying the dress is too good to have been made willy-nilly."

"It wasn't made willy-nilly." Eloise said with a smile. "I made it from an old dress."

"Well, now you're just poking fun at me and my whole profession."

Eloise might be laughing at snarky Bob, but Ricky's defenses roared again.

As if sensing that, she put her hand on his arm and calmed him as she faced Bob. "I'm going to take that as a compliment."

"And you should. Good grief, woman, you've got some talent there." He sucked in a breath. "I hope I'm not having dinner with my competition for next year."

Eloise laughed again, but Ricky looked from Bob to Eloise. He glanced at her gown, then back at Bob. His mouth fell open slightly. She might not be good enough to be Bob's competition, but something flashed through his brain. An insight. An intuition.

Maybe he should be introducing her to designers instead of CEOs. She might not have any human resources experience, but he'd seen her remake at least eight dresses. And she could sew. She was perfect intern material for a designer. In fact, he already knew the changes he'd make to her résumé. He could see himself selling her, getting her a job—a job she could not only do, but also probably like better than being stuck in a stuffy office.

His heart lightened but only for a second, then it dipped

with sorrow. The sooner he found her a job, the sooner he'd stop seeing her.

But she needed a job. And she needed to be away from him. He might be incredibly sad to lose their last few dates, but walking out of her life was the right thing to do.

He spent the first hour of dancing looking for designers he could waltz her in front of and failing miserably. He knew CEOs. He didn't know designers, except the one he'd lent money to.

Plus, he'd assumed she wanted to work with a designer. What if she didn't? He'd easily come to the conclusion this was what she should want, but until *she* realized it, he couldn't really change her résumé or send her on interviews.

Preoccupation with his mission kept him too busy to remember their attraction, too busy to regret that he couldn't have anything to do with her. But as they walked up the steps to her apartment at the end of the night, his chest tightened.

The closer they got to the spot where he'd kissed her, the more he remembered. The softness of her lips and the feeling that loving her was right closed in on him, stealing his breath.

He stopped after only two flights. "You know what?"

She faced him with a smile.

He worked up enough energy to return her smile but just barely. "I'm going to skip the second two flights of stairs tonight."

"Oh." He watched myriad emotions flutter through her soft blue eyes, but she said only, "Okay."

Still, when he turned to walk away, he knew he hadn't fooled her. She realized he was dodging a kiss. A kiss she wanted. A kiss he wanted.

The urge to pivot again and yank her into his arms spiked. He could kiss her senseless in thirty seconds. He could take command, take control, love her the way she deserved to be loved—and ultimately hurt her.

He kept walking.

Eloise stepped into her dark apartment, once again regretting that she didn't have anyone to talk to. He'd pulled back so far it was as if their kiss hadn't happened, and she wondered about the wisdom of not calling him on it, demanding he explain how he could be so affectionate one night and so distant the next.

She ambled to her room, her dress swishing, her spirits struggling to remember that she'd said she would give him time and that she had a job to do too.

She had to prove herself trustworthy. But how could a person prove herself trustworthy in a sea of people having fun? She couldn't. And when their dates were done, she would lose him.

The following Saturday night when Ricky picked her up for yet another formal party, his heart stumbled in his chest. He didn't know the proper name for the style of her dress and could only describe it as something he'd seen worn by ancient Greek goddesses in history books. Her hair piled on top of her head, with curls tickling her nape, also reminded him of a goddess.

If he'd thought he'd had trouble keeping his distance before, the way she looked tonight blew every other night out of the water.

He'd think himself in deep trouble, except her being beautiful in an exquisite dress actually worked for his plan. Instead of trying to search out designers, he'd stacked the deck. And he'd gotten the idea from Bob being seated with them accidentally the week before. This week, he'd called their hosts, the Connors, and asked for a favor.

He helped her up the few steps to the hotel. They smiled at the doorman and eased their way into the elevator. They'd taken only three steps into the ballroom when Jason Grogin caught his arm. "Hey! Ricky! Good to see you."

He shook Jason's hand, not quite as happy to see Jason as Jason seemed to be to see him. Jason was one of the people Ricky had originally sent Eloise's résumé to. And neither one of them had heard a word from him—in spite of the fact that he owed Ricky a huge favor.

Instead of, "Good to see you, too," Ricky merely said, "Jason."

Jason faced Eloise. "And this must be Eloise Vaughn."

"Yes." She shot Ricky a questioning look as Jason shook her hand.

"Your résumé landed in my in-box a few weeks ago, but I have to apologize for being out of town."

Her face lit. "You've been out of town?"

"Yes. So I didn't see Ricky's email until yesterday." He smiled. "I'd hoped we'd run into each other tonight." He caught Ricky's gaze. "We do have a job for you."

Eloise all but jumped for joy. "You do!"

He handed her a business card. "I spoke with my human resources person today, and she penciled you in for an interview after the holidays. It's just a formality, mostly about having the correct paperwork for our files. As far as I'm concerned, you're our newest employee. Assistant to the director. Who, I might add, is in her sixties and will probably be looking to retire in four or five years."

Eloise's mouth fell open. "Oh, my God! Thank you."

Jason smiled. "You're welcome." He slapped Ricky's back. "Enjoy the party."

Ricky said, "Thanks," but the muscle in his jaw twitched. "It's just like him to waltz up to us weeks later and offer you a job."

Eloise blinked. "I don't care if he was late." She caught his arm. "You did it! You got me a job!"

He should have been happy. His debt was paid. Instead, annoyance rattled through him. He'd finally seen what was right before his eyes all along—that Eloise had chosen the wrong career—but before he could get her in front of a designer who would realize her talents, Jason's offer would spoil it.

He found their table and pulled out her chair just as Artie Best pulled out the chair across the table for his date, a pouting redhead, undoubtedly a model.

Ricky smiled. The Connors had come through. This battle wasn't over yet.

As he sat, he motioned to Artie. "Eloise, I'd like you to meet Artie Best."

Her eyes grew, as he'd hoped they would. "Artie Best of Artie Best Dresses?"

Artie laughed. "The same. Still trying to get as popular as Jimmy Choo of Jimmy Choo shoes. But my name doesn't have quite the ring."

"Oh, your name rings fine with me." She sighed dreamily. "Your fall collection knocked me out."

His eyes narrowed unhappily. "Then why are you wearing someone else's gown?"

Eloise glanced down at her royal blue dress.

Glad he'd reacted the same way jealous Bob Barbie had, Ricky jumped in. "She's not wearing someone else. She's a designer herself. She's wearing her own dress."

"No kidding?" More businessman than Bob, Artie stood and motioned for her to do the same. "Let me take a look."

With a quick glance at Ricky, she rose cautiously.

Ricky slid his chair back so Artie could get a full view. But he hadn't needed to. Artie wasn't shy about pulling her away from the table and turning her around so he could examine all sides of her gown.

"I have to admit I've noticed you before."

She blinked at him. "You have?"

"Yes. You wore two dresses that were almost identical." He smiled. "The ones with no back."

She laughed. "The style is kind of a crowd favorite."

Artie said, "With your behind I have no doubt."

Ricky rose. "You know, Eloise is looking for a job."

"Really?"

"She has a degree in human resources, and though that probably doesn't translate into design, I think it's pretty clear she has talent."

Eloise faced him, her eyes round and questioning. "And no experience in fashion or design!"

Artie batted a hand. "Oh, please. Did you sew this?"

"Yes."

"Then you have experience." He turned her around for one more look at the blue gown. "I'm going to the Bahamas for the holidays, but I'd love to talk to you about coming to work for me when I get back."

"That'll be too late," Ricky said, helping Eloise to sit again as Artie walked back to his chair. "She has an interview with a company for an HR job and her rent is due."

Eloise's mouth fell open and her eyes flashed fire, but Artie laughed. "Working girls, right, sweetie?" He squeezed the shoulders of his beautiful red-haired date who looked totally bored with the conversation. "I remember the days when rent was a problem." He sighed, pulled out a card and wrote on the back. He handed it to Eloise. "That's my office. I'm leaving for the Bahamas tomorrow afternoon, but if you get there by eight tomorrow morning, I can run you through some paces."

Eloise blinked at him. "I...I..."

"She'll be there," Ricky said. "I'll have Norman drive her."

"Great."

Eloise didn't know whether to laugh or groan. She'd spent two years all but starving, desperate for a job, and finally she had a job, and Ricky didn't seem to want her to take it.

As soon as they got on the dance floor, away from the

table full of designers they'd been seated with, she pounced. "What are you doing?"

Looking smug and handsome, he said, "What am I doing about what?"

"I got a job and you totally disregarded that and got me an interview."

"An interview for a job I think you're much better qualified for."

"Designing?"

"Or learning the ropes in a low-level position that'll get your foot in the door of the industry where your talents really lie."

She gaped at him. "Life isn't about talent. It's about skill."

"And you have the skills." He glanced down at her. "What are you afraid of?"

With her gaze holding his, her pulse stuttered. *I'm afraid of you. I'm so in love with you my heart hurts. But you want me to prove myself and I don't know how. And we're just about out of time. That's what I'm afraid of.*

Instead, she looked away and said, "I went off on my own once before, remember? Followed my heart. Married a guy I loved. And it ended abysmally."

"Yeah, it did."

"Yet you want me to follow my heart again?"

"Yeah, I do."

"Did you ever stop to think that you don't get a vote?"

"Of course I don't. But I know you. And I think of you like a friend."

Her gaze met his again. That was what he'd said the night at the hospital. *Friendship. Not love—*

Oh, Lord. Had she made too much out of that kiss? She knew he'd felt something. She'd thought she only needed to prove herself, but what if he really did just think of her as a friend?

"You have more energy and enthusiasm than my staff

all put together. But not for business…" He winced. "For your clothes. I don't mean to insult you or trivialize it, but I think you'd have more fun in fashion."

She glanced away. What had she expected? That he'd say, "I love you. That's why I want you to be in the job where you're more suited? That's why I want you to be happy?" The man was wounded. He'd trusted a woman who didn't deserve trusting. He might have kissed her with real emotion, but after that he'd shut down. She'd thought all she had to do was prove herself, but what if he'd shut down because he simply didn't want her?

Or what if that kiss hadn't been as good to him as it had been to her? What if that was why he was back to calling her his friend?

Disappointment choked her, but her pride surfaced to save her. She would not make a fool of herself in front of him again.

Although every fiber in her being wanted to weep, she took a long, slow breath to compose herself and quietly said, "I probably would have more fun in fashion." She glanced at him again. "But would I be able to eat?"

"Eventually."

She laughed. Dear God, the man was honest. Here she was ready to fall into a black pit of despair and he didn't sugarcoat her situation. Of course, he probably didn't realize she was drowning. That she had fallen in love and he hadn't.

"If there's one thing I like about you, it's that you speak your mind."

"I do. My guess is you'd have a year as a gopher of some sort and years of apprenticing, but at least this time your sacrifices would have a goal. And someday you might make it big. Maybe start your own line."

"My own line? Isn't that a little ambitious?"

"Not if you have an investor behind you. Someone who knows your work and likes you."

Her eyes sought his again. His gaze didn't waver.

OMG. Had he just admitted he liked her? That he wanted to stay in her life? With their Christmas deal ending, was he looking for a way to continue to see her?

"You'd do that?"

"We'd have to see how you progress under Artie's tutelage, but, yeah, I'd do that."

She stared at him, her eyes drowning in fresh tears. Her chest swelled with hope. Designing her own line was a dream come true, but the hope came from staying in his life. He wasn't leaving her. He was making a place for her so that he could take his time.

They had time.

"Look. Go to the interview tomorrow or don't. It's your choice. But at least know you have a choice."

She licked her suddenly dry lips. "Yes. I do."

The music stopped and the couple next to them walked over. Ricky shook the man's hand and introduced him to Eloise as Steve Grant, a Wall Street guy, and his wife, Amanda, a lawyer. She smiled politely and nodded and agreed when it seemed appropriate, but her head was swimming.

In the space of an hour, her entire life—all her goals—had changed, but all she could focus on was the fact that she'd see him again. He was making room for her in his life, a reason for them to see each other for however long he invested in her.

Her brain froze. *For as long as he invested in her?*

Had he turned their relationship into another business deal?

CHAPTER TEN

THEY RODE HOME in absolute silence. On the one hand, she didn't want to lose him, and staying connected meant they'd continue to see each other. On the other, if his offer was only a business deal, she might have already lost him.

At her apartment door, he said, "So, you're okay with everything?"

Okay? She wasn't even sure she understood it. But she did want the interview. And she did understand that even if Ricky didn't love her, he'd done more than provide job opportunities for her. He'd gone the extra mile and helped her find what she really wanted to do with the rest of her life.

She couldn't dismiss that or belittle it.

"I'm ecstatic. I wouldn't have even attempted getting an apprentice job with someone like Artie Best." She caught his gaze. "Thanks. Really."

He smiled. "I'll send Norman tomorrow morning to drive you to the interview."

Confusion poured through her. He'd almost kissed her on their tequila night. He'd kissed her with unbearable emotion the night of their carriage ride. He'd understood something about her and her career that she hadn't even realized herself. Yet he was so distant she had no choice but to believe that sending his car for her was only an extension of their deal.

"You don't have to do that. I'll take the subway."

He stopped her by putting his hand on her shoulder. "It's Norman's job to know how to get places. He'll do the research tonight to find Artie's offices. That way you can relax and spend your mental energy preparing for the interview."

Because that made sense, she nodded. "Thanks."

Although his hand was on her shoulder, he didn't try to bring her close for a kiss. Hell, he didn't look one bit like a man who wanted to kiss her. He just squeezed lightly, turned and started down the hall. "Good night."

She swallowed. Emptiness tightened her chest. Even if she got a position with Artie Best, and—years down the road—Ricky decided to invest in her designs, he could pass her off to assistants. This might be the last time she ever saw him, and she was looking at his back as he walked away.

Her voice a confused whisper, she said, "Good night."

"I'll see you tomorrow afternoon."

Her breath stumbled. "Tomorrow afternoon?"

He faced her again. "For my office party."

She blinked.

"You can tell me how the interview went then. In fact, why don't we just have Norman bring you to my office after the interview, save some time?"

Her heart fell. He just wanted to hear about her morning with Artie Best. "But I'll be dressed for an interview, not a party."

He shrugged. "My employees are coming to the office on an afternoon they don't have to, so it's informal. Jeans. Sweaters. You'll be fine."

He headed for the stairs, and she walked into her apartment. They might be going to another party, but he hadn't wanted to kiss her and he had gotten her a job. Even if he continued their deal, they only had one more party and one wedding.

How the heck was she supposed to prove herself in two events? Especially when it was clear he was distancing himself.

As promised, bright and early Sunday morning, Norman texted her that he was outside her apartment building. In skinny jeans, tall black boots and her beloved green cashmere sweater, she slid into her parka and scrambled down the stairs.

Norman awaited her at the door to the limo.

"Good morning."

He smiled. "Good morning."

She slid inside and he got behind the steering wheel. When the car began to move, he opened the glass that separated them.

"I'm hoping you have good luck on your interview."

She laughed. "Yeah. Me too. There's only so long a person can live on noodles before they start feeling like a big bowl of chicken soup."

Catching her gaze in the mirror, he grinned. "I like you. You're not Mr. Langley's typical date."

"He likes them richer?"

"He used to like them poutier."

"Used to?"

"He hasn't dated in a long time. But when he dated, the women he chose were rich and spoiled, or models or starlets, women accustomed to attention." He smiled in the mirror again. "You're their opposite."

She didn't have the heart to tell him Ricky dating her had been a ruse. Her soul was so sad that the only thing keeping her going this morning was the knowledge that she might get a job in the fashion industry. Not in a stuffy office, but at a place where she'd help design the clothes the rest of the world would wear.

It wasn't quite a magical end to her dating a man she

accidentally fell in love with, but it was heady stuff, and she would appreciate it.

So she pasted on a smile for Norman and said, "Thank you."

"No. Thank you. And good luck."

Although his thank you puzzled her, through the rest of the ride she focused her attention on what she'd say to Artie Best. For once, she wasn't going to an interview hoping for rent money. She *wanted* this job. *Wanted* this career. She would have to be sharp to get it.

Artie Best's office was the top floor of an old factory. Quirky and fun, it was filled with fabric and dress molds, sewing machines and drafting tables. Racks of dresses lined the entire side wall.

"This place is great."

He ushered her to a small room in the back. "We like it."

As he sat on the chair behind a big metal desk, he motioned for her to take the seat in front of it. "So you haven't been to design school?"

She shook her head. "No. Sorry."

He inclined his head. "I didn't go either."

Her spirits rose a bit. "You didn't?"

"No, but I apprenticed." He sat back. "Your boyfriend's a very wealthy, influential man."

The heat of embarrassment filled her. She had to struggle not to tell Artie Best that Ricky wasn't her boyfriend. If he was only hiring her to get in good with Ricky, it wouldn't get him very far. But if she admitted the truth to Artie Best, then she'd be betraying Ricky.

Still, she couldn't quite hold her tongue, couldn't deceive him into thinking he'd be getting something he wasn't. "I'm only here because you want to get in good with Ricky?"

"No. You're here because you have talent. What I'm telling you is that I don't do favors for rich guys. If you think dating Ricky Langley will get you special treatment, then this interview can be over. If you think dating Ricky Langley means you don't have to apprentice, you know the way to the door. But if you want a real career in this industry, if you don't mind hard work and a learning curve…then I really do want to talk."

Four hours later, she all but skipped out of Artie's building onto the street to Norman, who held open the limo door.

"You got it?"

She beamed. "Yes!"

"Very good."

He closed the door and slid onto the front seat, started the engine and drove off.

She leaned back on the soft leather, her heart pounding, her spirits lifted in a way they hadn't been in five years. She didn't have a goal anymore. She had a vision. She could see herself working for Artie, learning, squirreling away information and experience until one day she could be her own boss. Have her own line.

Her own line.

Even the thought stole her breath.

Norman pulled the limo up to the curb in front of a tall white office building. She danced inside, pushed the button for the floor listed for Ricky's suite in the building directory and rode the elevator, trying to school her face so Ricky's employees wouldn't think she was drunk or high or just plain crazy.

The doors opened on a reception area. A black marble security station looped around in a huge semicircle. A pleasant security guard greeted her.

"Can I help you, miss?"

"I'm Eloise Vaughn, Mr. Langley's friend. I'm here for the Christmas party."

He studied a list on a tablet screen and frowned. "I'm sorry. I don't see your name."

A week ago that would have thrown her for a loop. Her

pride would have taken a direct hit. Knowing Ricky had forgotten her, she would have slunk away.

Today? Nothing could stop her. The hurts of the last five years had been tidily tucked away. She was a new person now. A woman with a job and a vision. A woman who wasn't afraid to stand up for herself.

A woman who wasn't letting the love of her life go without a fight.

She struggled not to gasp. When had that happened? And when had she gotten her boldness back?

She didn't know. Maybe the excitement of finally finding her way had filled her with strength. But whatever it was, it felt right.

Wayne might have been a love in her life, but Ricky was *the* great love of her life. She wasn't losing him.

She smiled at the security guard. "Give him a call. Tell him Eloise is here and I'm not on your list."

He hesitated.

"Don't be afraid. He really did invite me."

Skeptical, the security guard picked up the receiver of the black phone on the desk. He pressed a button.

"Mr. Langley, I'm sorry to bother you, but there's a woman at the desk...an Eloise..." He grimaced. "Yes. Thank you." He hung up the phone and smiled at Eloise. "You can go back."

She headed to the glass doors that led to a cubicle canyon, but she stopped. "What about you?"

The guard faced her. "Excuse me?"

"What about you? Don't you get to go to the party?"

"The guards take turns manning the security desk. We go into the party in shifts."

From his place in the back of the huge one-room main office of his company, Ricky watched Eloise open the door, then pause and talk to the security guard. Concern for the young man was written all over her face.

He shook his head. She was such a sweet, consider-ate person that the thought of losing her rocketed sadness through him. She was different from any woman he'd dated, any woman he knew—except Olivia. But wouldn't it make sense that friends like Olivia and Eloise would share the same traits? Honesty. Integrity. Kindness.

Or maybe, knowing her and Olivia, he was finally com-ing to realize all women weren't like his ex. He'd never date another party girl again, but there were plenty of good women in the world. Eloise being one of the best.

Still, the fact that Eloise was so good, so wonderful, made it imperative that he not drag her into his depress-ing life. So this would be their last day together. Their last party. If she'd gotten the job, there was no reason to pro-long the agony. If he wanted to remember her, he would have to drink in every detail today because he'd never see her again.

She walked past gray cubicle walls draped with tinsel, under the big red holiday ornament that hung from the cen-ter of the ceiling and by the ledges of windows that held evergreen branches sprayed with fake snow.

He knew the second she saw him because she smiled and waved. His heart flip-flopped as he motioned for her to join him.

She all but skipped over to the copy machine where he stood. Adding that skip to the light in her eyes told the whole story. She'd gotten the job.

Not wanting to spoil her moment, he said, "Well?"

"I got it!"

"I knew it."

She unexpectedly rose to her tiptoes and hugged him tightly.

His heart tripped over itself in his chest. He longed to take her face in his hands and kiss her. Hard. But that would only confuse things. Or make him pine for things he couldn't have. He squeezed his eyes shut and for a few seconds enjoyed the feeling of her arms around him. Then he stepped back.

"What are we going to do about your gifts?"

He glanced up to see David giving him a curious look. And why not? This time last year, he couldn't even attend this party. This year, he'd doubled bonuses, come to the party and had just been hugged by a pretty girl.

Still, none of his assistants had mentioned gifts. "What gifts?"

Tall, gray-haired David shifted uneasily. "Well, because this is a party, I thought it might be cute to put the bonus envelopes into little gift boxes. That kind of morphed into buying everybody a watch."

He frowned, but Eloise tugged on his arm. "It *is* cute."

That was one of the reasons he liked her. He thought like a guy. Logical. Straightforward. She was more of a people person. Now that she'd had approved it, he supposed tucking bonuses into watch boxes was cute.

"Okay."

David smiled at Eloise and she smiled back, as if they shared some great secret.

"I think everybody will love it."

"So I just have to hand out gifts?"

David winced. "Well, there is one teeny tiny other thing you could do to make this party really fun."

He sighed. "What?"

David glanced at Eloise, then quickly back at Ricky before he said, "Would you mind putting on the Santa suit?"

His face fell. His heart stuttered. The one and only time he'd worn the Santa suit he'd had Blake at this party.

Eloise touched his arm again. "I think that would be cute, too."

He swallowed.

Obviously reading his reaction, David shook his head. "Don't worry about it. I just got carried away."

Ricky caught Eloise's gaze again. She tilted her head and smiled at him, encouraging him.

He wasn't ready. But something about the way she looked at him emboldened him. At some point, he had to get back into life—or at least pretend to get back into life so his employees could stop worrying. After he gave out the gifts, the party would be over. His employees would go to the bar down the street. It wasn't like he had to be Santa for hours. Just twenty minutes.

Surely, he could do that?

"Okay." He looked Eloise again. "But she has to be the elf."

"Elf?" She laughed.

David beamed at Eloise. "Love it! Follow me."

They walked back to David's office and he pulled two big boxes from a closet. He smiled broadly as he handed Eloise the top box. "You can change in the ladies' room just down the hall." He handed the fatter box to Ricky. "You can just change here."

With that he left the office. Eloise followed on his heels.

Ten minutes later, Ricky was in his fat suit when Eloise returned from the ladies' room dressed in green tights, a short red dress and a long green hat that had a jingle bell that bounced off her shoulder when she walked.

"This is weird."

She looked cute. Happy. Like Christmas spirit personified. Everything in him filled with joy, reminding him of the incredible happiness that swirled through his parents' house at the holidays.

He jerked himself back to reality. Where had that memory come from? Why had looking at Eloise made him think of his parents?

"You should be me." He adjusted the fat pack at his belly. "I feel like a couch pillow."

She laughed.

And his heart lifted again. She obviously loved Christmas, and making her laugh suddenly felt like it should be his life's mission.

He sucked in a breath, confused by his jumbled thoughts. Especially because that last one was just wrong. It couldn't be his mission to make anyone happy. He was too depressed.

He picked up the sack of presents David had left behind. "I can't believe I agreed to do this again."

"You've done it before?"

He took a long breath, wondering why he always spoke before he thought with her. "Once." He shook his head, again dislodging unwanted memories that flooded his brain. Memories of Blake this time. Christmas in his penthouse. Sneaking into the living room to plug in the tree lights so that when he carried Blake into the room everything would be perfect.

Everything had been perfect.

His breath stuttered out. His feeling of sadness returned. "It's not important. The important thing is you've got a job."

"A career," she interjected. "As I was explaining to Artie why he should hire me, I realized that even though I'm probably still going to starve for a few years, it will be sacrifice with a purpose. Exactly what you'd told me." She caught his gaze. "How'd you get so smart?"

He quickly looked away and hefted the heavy sack over his shoulder. "Part of being a leader is knowing where people fit. I'm amazed it took me so long to figure you out."

He pointed at the door. "Let's go. When the punch runs out, everybody goes to a little bar down the street. We need to give them their gifts before they desert us."

She opened the glass door of David's office and directed him down the hall.

"Ho! Ho! Ho!"

At Ricky's joyful call, the seventy or so employees scattered about in the cubicles stopped talking.

"Has everybody been a good employee?"

Eloise laughed gaily. The little bell at the end of her hat tinkled.

"This is my elf, Eloise." He paused and faced her. "Eloise Elf…it has a nice ring to it."

She rang her bell. "I think so."

Everybody laughed.

That strange feeling floated through Ricky again. This time he recognized it. Happiness. He told himself he didn't deserve it, but it didn't go away. Plus, it felt different. Strong. Weirdly strong. As if the earth had shifted and everything in his past was gone.

He shook his head. Everything in his past gone? He didn't *want* his past gone. He didn't want to forget his son. That was absurd.

He got himself back to the business at hand, distributing the bonuses hidden in gifts wrapped in bright red, green, blue, silver and gold foil paper.

Eloise handed him the first box. He read the name, and when the employee opened his gift—a watch—he also found an envelope. He ripped open the envelope, did a small dance of joy, raced over to his cubicle where he grabbed his coat and ran out.

Seeing the confused look on Eloise's face, Ricky leaned in. "Employee bonuses, remember?"

She turned to him and he realized he'd leaned in so far their faces were only inches apart.

"Oh?"

The temptation to kiss her stormed through him, knitting itself to that odd sensation that everything had shifted. But it couldn't have shifted. He couldn't change the past. He might love having her around, but she was better off without him.

He pulled away. "Some of the junior employees, people learning the ropes, earn just enough for their keep. This year, thanks to you, I realized they needed a better bonus."

She smiled. "You're a good guy."

Happiness fluttered through him, not because he thought himself good, but because he knew she genuinely believed it. It had been so long since anyone had thought of him as good—since *he* had thought of himself as good—that even stranger feelings rose up in him.

If they had been alone, he might have told her about Blake. Everything inside him longed to tell her, even though he could see no point to it. In a few hours, he'd never see her again. So maybe it was lucky this was the wrong place, the wrong time.

He handed out the gifts, and the reaction that rippled through the group made him laugh. Everyone came up and shook his hand. Some people told him what they intended to do with the unexpected extra money. Others just hugged him.

Christmas spirit warmed his heart, and he finally identified the odd feeling swimming through him. It wasn't happiness. After eighteen long months, he felt normal. He hadn't changed. The world hadn't shifted. He was simply coming back to the land of the living.

But he had also been correct. Once the punch ran out, his employees jetted off. A few suggested he join them at the pub. He politely declined.

With everyone gone, he walked through the room, gathering wayward wrapping paper and empty punch glasses.

Out of her elf suit and back in her jeans and sexy black boots, Eloise sat on a desk, watching him. "So now you clean up?"

"My mom always taught me to pick up empty glasses." He shook his head with a laugh. The memory of his happy childhood was so strong he couldn't banish it, and longing to be home filled his chest. "Old habits die hard."

"Oh, I don't know. It seems to me your mom taught you well. She sounds like a good person."

He hesitated. "She is." That funny feeling—the sense that he was reentering the land of the living—rattled through him again. He could see his mom and dad by the big Christmas tree in the great room of their log home. He could see his sisters with their kids and spouses. He could see the empty place in the crowd, by the mantel, where he should be standing.

Her laugh penetrated his haze. "Hey! Earth to Ricky."

He glanced up sharply. She sat on the desk, one leg tucked under her. A glass of punch in her hand. The gleam of success in her eyes.

He knew that he had Eloise to thank for the normal feeling that kept creeping up on him. And, although she was happy right now, she had no one. He might have gotten her a job, but she'd be alone on Christmas. It just wasn't right.

He ran his hand along the back of his neck. "Give me ten minutes to change out of this suit."

"Sure."

He raced down the hall. As he slipped out of his red flannel Santa clothes, he grabbed his cell phone and called David.

The noise of the pub poured through the phone when his assistant answered.

"I know you're celebrating, but I have a major mission for you." After the promise of another bonus, Ricky outlined his plan.

David laughed, but Ricky said, "Don't take this too lightly. This mission comes with a deadline. You have just a little more than one hour."

Norman drove them back to her apartment, and even to Eloise, who hoped to stall her time with Ricky, it seemed as if he took his time.

But eventually the silent ride came to an end. She wasn't surprised that Ricky shifted nervously as they climbed the several flights of stairs to her apartment. He hadn't made any mention of the Christmas Eve wedding she'd been expecting to attend with him. And she suspected this was it. Their last few minutes together.

When they finally reached her apartment door, he put his hand on her shoulder. "Mind if I come in?"

She met his gaze slowly, not sure why he wanted to come in. Would she get a kiss? An explanation? A sad goodbye? Or did he want a few minutes to remind her that in a few years, when she had some experience, he would fund her?

Her spirit of boldness rose up in her again. She was not letting him go without a fight. If he was giving her five minutes of private time, she would use them.

"I'd love for you to come in." She had no idea what she would do, but she wasn't going to just stand there, letting him go, letting him pretend there was nothing between them.

She turned, unlocked her door, opened it and stopped dead in her tracks.

Surrounding her pitiful eighteen-inch plastic tree were several boxes.

He leaned in, over her shoulder. "I think Santa's been here."

"*You're* Santa."

"Exactly."

He gave her a nudge into the apartment. "Go. Open them."

Not sure what was going on, she hesitantly walked over to the little tree. Sitting on the window seat, surrounded by cotton pretending to be snow, the plastic tree was dwarfed by one tall box, one huge box and three smaller ones.

Her chest tightened. All this time she'd been thinking she had to make a move to keep him. But maybe these gifts meant he was trying to keep her?

"Open the little ones first."

Confused, she slowly picked up the small square box to find a pink cashmere sweater. *Pink.* The color he'd liked her in the best.

Her gaze flew to his. "I love it."

He smiled. "I knew you would. Open the next small one."

She ripped the wrapping paper off a box that had clearly come from a jewelry store. "A diamond watch?"

Before she could say anything, he directed her to the last small box. "Keep going."

She opened the gift to find a book: *How to Get the Most Out of Your Intern Experience.*

She laughed. "I'll need this much more than a diamond watch."

He pointed at one of the two bigger boxes. Steeped in bewilderment, she opened this one a little slower. It contained a satin evening cape.

"Not a fur," he said, explaining his choice. "Something I think you'll be comfortable in. And look," he said, pointing out the quilted material beneath the shiny cape. "It has a lining for really cold nights."

She caught his gaze. He beamed at her. She'd never seen him so happy. As much as she wanted to ask him what the hell was going on, she couldn't spoil his fun. "It's perfect."

He pointed at the final box. "Now, the last one."

She ripped off the paper to reveal a shiny new coffee-maker. Her gaze swung to his.

"There's a year's supply of coffee too."

She said, "Thanks," but her voice choked. He'd gotten her coffee? Only a person who truly knew her, who paid attention to her, would know how much she'd missed her coffee. How could that possibly mean anything except that he loved her? Her eyes filled with tears.

"You don't like it?"

So why didn't he just say he loved her?

"Everything is perfect."

"Over the past few weeks you've given me lots of gifts. The biggest one was happiness."

She looked at him, her eyes blurry with tears. *Just let him say it. Please let him say it!*

"You changed me. I was stuck. I couldn't even see a speck of light at the end of any tunnel. All I saw was darkness until you. Then gradually I started seeing things differently again, and today I realized I felt normal."

Her confusion returned. "You feel normal?"

"Yes. Not perfect, certainly not good, but normal."

"So you bought me a bunch of gifts?"

"Important gifts. Things I know you'll need."

Confusion and pain collided to create an indescribable tightness in her chest. She was expecting him to tell her he loved her and instead he'd bought her gifts to show his appreciation.

But they were important gifts.

Gifts that proved he knew her and cared enough about her that he bought the things she really needed. He *had* to love her. Nothing else made sense.

She slowly met his gaze. "You have to help me out here." She lifted the new evening coat. "What does this mean?"

"It means you no longer have to wear your wool cape."

She shook her head fiercely. "No. Don't cop out. The real bottom line to all these gifts is that you know me. You *like* me."

He nodded. "I do."

"So do these gifts mean we're dating for real?"

"Oh, Eloise." He shook his head. "You wouldn't want that."

Her heart kicked with fear. After everything they'd shared, how could he not see they were made for each other? How could he believe she wouldn't want him?

"I would! I *do*!"

"You don't."

She set the coffeemaker on the sofa and scrambled over to stand beside him. When he turned to walk way, she caught his arm, forced him to face her.

"Tell me why. After all these weeks of dating, getting close, why are you pushing me away?"

He didn't even try to deny that he was pushing her away. "Because I'm no good for you."

"That's another cop-out. Another vague reason that explains nothing!"

"Be glad I'm not letting you in." He pivoted, motioning with his arms to the gifts and wrapping paper. "Christmas kills me."

"Hey, it's not exactly a walk in the park for me either. I'm alone. I lost a husband and have no family. You can't tell me not seeing your son is worse."

He stared at her, his mouth slightly open. "How can you say that?"

"I know it's painful. I think it's unconscionable that your ex took him away—"

He gaped at her. "My ex didn't take him away."

"She didn't?"

He squeezed his eyes shut, then popped them open again. "No, Eloise. He died. My son, Blake, died."

Her brain froze. Her breathing stalled. Incomprehension stopped her heart. "Your son is *dead.*"

He said nothing.

White-hot anger fueled the pain that roared through her. "Your son is *dead*...and you didn't tell me?"

"I didn't want your pity."

"Pity?"

"I always told you that. I wanted you to behave normally at those parties. To make it look like we were beyond my tragedy. And it worked. I could even play Santa today."

The shock and pain that filled her nearly burst her chest. She fell to the sofa, feeling like a hundred different kinds of fool. But most of all, she just felt sad. He hadn't trusted her enough to tell her the most important fact of his life.

He didn't love her.

She loved him, but he clearly didn't love her.

He scrubbed his hand across his mouth. "Look, I'm sorry. But I needed this. I really, really needed a few weeks of pretending I was okay."

She said nothing. The pain of knowing he didn't love her, that he probably didn't feel anything for her, was too intense.

"Blake was eighteen months old. He and his mother had been at a barbecue. She wrecked her car, a convertible. She hit a pole...and Blake was thrown from her car. He lived for only forty-eight more hours."

She went from upset to horror so quickly her breath caught.

"You want to know the worst of it? Had Blake been buckled into his car seat properly, he would have been fine." He took a breath and turned to Eloise. "His mother had been drinking. She wasn't sloshed, but her blood alcohol was over the legal limit. And she hadn't buckled him in right."

"She didn't want him. Never had. She wanted eighteen years' worth of child support. I have no doubt that she loved Blake. But she wasn't a mother. I saw the signs." He squeezed his eyes shut. "I saw a hundred signs. And I wanted Blake. I had a weekend nanny I could have hired permanently. I had the big penthouse. I had the money. But I always thought I'd talk to her about my taking custody the next weekend or the next or the next." He faced her sad Christmas tree again. "Now Blake is dead and his mother is serving out a manslaughter sentence."

Eloise caught his gaze as a bit of understanding crept in. His story wasn't just a story of loss. It was a story of failure. And guilt. Pain. Shame. Torment. He believed his son's death was his fault.

Her anger dissolved in the face of her love for him. Not quite sure what to say, she slowly rose from the sofa. "You can't change the past. But that doesn't mean you should stop living."

He spun to face her. "It doesn't?" He laughed harshly. "Really? Because there are some days I think stopping living would be easier. My son is dead. It *is* my fault. I deal with that every day."

"Of course, you do. But you just told me I gave you eleven dates of happiness. You're on the right track."

"I'm on no track. I take one day at a time, bury myself in work. It's all I have. All I deserve."

Her fight returned. Something inside told her if she didn't reach him now, she wouldn't get another chance. "I know it's hard to see right now, but you deserve more. A lot more."

His voice softened. She could almost see defeat settle on his shoulders. "No. I don't."

She sucked in a breath. The do-or-die feeling flooded her, urging her forward. "It doesn't matter what you think you deserve because I already love you."

"Then you're a fool." He walked over and slid his hands up her arms, as if comforting her. "You are a wonderful, beautiful woman who deserves to be pampered and loved. Getting involved with me would be nothing but sorrow for you."

Before she could stop him, he scooped his jacket off her sofa and walked out. Eloise raced after him, but he was so much faster than she was that by the time she reached the lobby, Norman was already pulling away from the curb.

He wasn't ever coming back. She'd never see him again.

Her chest stung. Her eyes filled with tears.

As always with him, she didn't feel her own pain. She felt his. Only this time it was stronger, like a coal from the burning pits of hell. His son was dead. He felt responsible for the imprisonment of a woman he shouldn't feel sorry for. He took too much on his shoulders.

It was no wonder he didn't want another wounded person in his life.

CHAPTER ELEVEN

THAT NIGHT RICKY couldn't settle. He had a bottle of Scotch, a glass and some ice, but he didn't feel like drinking. He didn't want to pace. He couldn't sit and mope. He had too much energy.

Energy.

He shook his head, lifted the Scotch and poured himself two fingers.

But though he brought the glass to his lips, he didn't drink it.

Everything felt off, wrong.

He walked to the back wall of the main room of his condo and stared at the decorated windows in the middle-class building across the street. He thought about his parents' huge log house, how good it looked decorated for the holidays. He closed his eyes, remembering the feeling he'd had that afternoon at the Christmas party. Eloise had been a perfect elf. His employees had been so happy that it fed something in him. And he'd remembered things about Christmases past. Things before Blake. Things that felt right. Good.

He thought about Eloise, sad at her apartment, and shook his head. It was for her benefit that he'd left her. This time next year she'd probably be so happy she wouldn't even remember he existed.

His chest tightened a bit at the thought, but he knew she deserved better, and he forced his mind off her.

His gaze landed on the pretty decorations in the windows of the building across the street again and he suddenly, overwhelmingly missed his parents. He might have to let Eloise go, but his parents were stuck with him. They had to let him into their lives.

He chuckled a bit. That was how he'd thought before Blake.

Maybe Eloise was right. Maybe she had been good for him. He might not be able to have a love in his life, a commitment, but it was time to let his parents in again.

He picked up his phone and called his mother.

After a short conversation, he called his pilot and arranged to fly home. Twenty minutes later, he reached into his closet for his leather jacket. But remembering the temperatures by the lakes in December, he changed his mind and took out his old navy blue parka. It should have reminded him of his last trip home, of taking Blake down a snowy slope on a saucer sled. Instead, he thought of Eloise. She'd worn a parka like this one to his fraternity reunion. As old and beat-up as the coat he pulled from the closet, her parka was undoubtedly as warm as this one.

And if there was one thing he knew about Eloise, it was that she was nothing if not practical.

He cursed as he shrugged into the coat, telling himself to forget about Eloise. About the pain that sliced through him at the thought of never seeing her again. About the emptiness that had filled his chest as he'd walked away from her. The unmet needs he knew she could fill. He would not saddle her with his life.

In his plane, he tucked earphones in his ears, put his seat back and listened to the soothing sounds of the ocean for only about ten minutes before the rhythm of the plane put him to sleep. He slept the full hour-long flight.

He wished his crew happy holidays and they thanked

him for the generous bonuses he'd given them for flying so close to Christmas. As he walked down the three steps to the tarmac, he saw his dad's old beat-up SUV sitting by the hangar of the private airstrip.

Wearing a brown work coat and boots, his dad leaned on the front fender, huddled against the howling wind that blew snow around him. He waved and joy stuttered through Ricky. He jogged down the steps, duffel bag in hand and walked over. His dad enveloped him in a hug.

"Your mom is so happy you're coming home that you better not tell us this is a two-hour visit."

He laughed and clasped his dad's shoulder. "Nope. I took two weeks. The staff has Christmas week off, but I decided I needed a rest."

His dad took a step back, studied his face. "You don't look tired. I expected you to look tired."

"I slept on the plane."

"Yeah, yeah, yeah," Jim Langley said as he rounded the hood of his SUV. "I get that you slept. But I'm not talking about sleepy tired. You've been away so long, I expected you to look worn down."

He opened the SUV door, tossed his duffel bag into the back and slid onto the passenger's side seat. "I've been coming around. Getting my energy back. Feeling a little better about things."

"So your mother said." He started the vehicle. "Time heals all wounds."

"This wound won't ever heal."

His father was quiet for a minute, then he said, "Maybe you don't want it to heal. You lost your son. Your first child. One of our precious grandchildren. We'll always remember him." His dad took his eyes off the road for a second to spear Ricky with a look over his glasses. "But life has to go on."

"Yeah. It might take me awhile to get there." If he ever got there at all, but he wouldn't burden his dad with that.

"Well, we're glad you're home."

They finished the drive to the house talking about the price of grapes and competition from a new vineyard. Ricky's eyes misted when he saw the huge log ranch house. Colorful Christmas lights blinked from evergreens that lined the lane and rimmed the wide front porch.

His dad grabbed his bag before Ricky was even out of his seat belt. By the time he came around to the side of the SUV facing the house, his mom was on the porch. She met him on the steps, hugged him so tightly he lost his breath, then pushed him away.

"Let me look at you."

His dad said, "He doesn't look tired."

"No. He doesn't." She studied his face again, then hooked her arm through his to walk him into the house.

Memories of Eloise hooking her arm through his before they entered a ballroom flooded him. He could see her take a breath, put a smile on her face and walk into the room as if she owned it.

"So? Coffee? Tea?"

Snapped out of his thoughts, Ricky faced his mom.

"Your dad's taken your bag upstairs." She grinned. "I made snickerdoodles, and your sisters should be here any minute with their kids."

He shrugged out of his coat. "I thought they didn't come over until Christmas morning."

His mom batted a hand. "Are you kidding? They couldn't wait. They're dying to see you." She leaned over and kissed his cheek. "You're the best gift we're all getting this Christmas."

He thought of Eloise again. If she dared go to her parents' house, she stood a good chance of getting rejected. Yet here he was, being told his visit was his family's best gift.

His mother tapped his arm. "You say you're getting better, but you keep leaving me."

He smiled. "Thinking about something."

"That's what worries me."

"It's not what you suspect." He glanced around the up-dated house that still retained its rustic log cabin feel. A huge tree stood in front of the window. Garland looped across the fireplace mantel. Candy canes lined the rim of a bowl full of nuts and chocolates. Eloise would love this.

"I have a friend." He cleared his throat. "Actually a friend of Olivia's who needed help finding a job. We spent time together to...well, fix her résumé among other things, and while we did she told me about her family."

Her mother tilted her head in question.

He shook his head, trying to dislodge thoughts of Elo-ise, especially because he couldn't explain her.

"Did she help you feel better?"

"Yes." This he could answer. "Assisting her was a big part of why I feel better."

"And did she tell you about her good family Christmases and how you needed family? Is that why you suddenly de-cided to come home?"

He winced. "Just the opposite. Her family sounds abys-mal." He cleared his throat again. "I guess she made me realize how lucky I have it."

"And you gave her a job?"

"No." He laughed. "She said she wouldn't take a job with me because she didn't want everybody at the office thinking she'd only gotten her job because we'd gone out."

His mother fell to the chair behind her. "You went out?"

From the stairs, his dad incredulously said, "On a date?"

Seeing they were getting the wrong idea, he said, "On eleven dates. But not like you think. I needed someone to go with me to my events so everybody would think I was fine—not grieving anymore—and stop worrying about me. We traded. She went to my parties, and I worked with her to find her a job."

Walking over to the sofa, his dad laughed. "You went out with the same woman eleven times?"

What was so weird about that? "Yes." He looked from his mother to his father. "She's very pretty and very nice and we got along very well."

His mother said, "Huh."

"She had a tragedy in her life, too. She'd married young and her husband died." He winced. "From cancer. She nursed him through his last months."

His dad shook his head. "She sounds like a very nice woman."

"She is. Losing her husband really hurt her, but to make matters worse, her family deserted her because her marriage had embarrassed them."

His dad's face contorted with disbelief. "What kind of family does that?"

"Like I said—a bad one."

His mother straightened on her chair. "So what's she doing for Christmas?"

He swallowed. "I'm not sure."

His dad frowned. "Let me get this straight. You went out with a woman eleven times. Because she had as difficult of a past as yours, you talked enough that she helped you get your bearings about Blake. Yet she told you she had a bad family, probably nowhere to go for Christmas and..." He caught Ricky's gaze. "You left alone?"

"It's complicated."

His mother rose. "No. It's not." She walked over to his chair and stooped in front of him. "Do you think just anybody can bring you around?"

He frowned.

His dad shook his head. "Son, you love this woman."

"I don't. I mean, yes, we were good together. We talked. She talked me through a lot."

"What did she say when you told her about Blake?"

He swallowed. "That she loved me."

His mother slapped his arm. "Well, you fool! She told you that she loves you. You talked to her about something you've never spoken about with us, and you don't think you love her?"

He licked his suddenly dry lips. He could see Eloise's face, the pain in her eyes when he walked away. But he could also see the happiness in her eyes on tequila night. The way she looked standing at that door, begging him for a kiss...the feelings that tumbled through him as he fought not to kiss her. The desire to be held by her. To belong to her.

Oh, my God.

"I—"

The door opened and his two sisters, their husbands and four kids poured in. After coats were removed and hung, he was enveloped in hugs. And the whole time his mouth stayed open as one truth blinked over and over and over in his brain like a Christmas light stuck in blink mode.

He loved her.

He pulled away from a particularly emotional hug from his sister. It all made sense now. That's why he had wanted to tell her about Blake. Why telling her hadn't broken his heart.

She had opened the door for him to move on.

The question was...could he?

Eloise awakened to the ring of her cell phone. She bounced up in bed, realized it was Christmas, and the deathly silence of her apartment closed in on her.

She was alone.

Ricky didn't want her.

The pain in her heart became like a great, throbbing weight.

The phone rang again.

Maybe Ricky had changed his mind? She'd made her case. She'd seen the sadness in his eyes when he'd left—

She grabbed the phone.

But Tucker and Olivia's engagement picture appeared on her screen.

Her heart swelled from disappointment. But she chastised herself. These were friends who truly loved her. If nothing else, she'd always have Tucker and Olivia. And Laura Beth would call.

She might not have the person she loved, but she really wasn't *alone.*

She cleared her throat, then swallowed back her tears before she clicked the button. "Hey, Merry Christmas!"

"Merry Christmas!"

The chorus that rang out to her was from Olivia's entire family. Her chest shivered from the desire to cry.

"Did you get the Christmas cookies?" Olivia's mom called.

"Yes!" She squeezed her eyes shut and swallowed back tears. She'd been in Olivia's parents' house enough that she could picture the cozy living room, stockings on the fireplace mantel, a fat awkward tree in the corner brimming with blinking lights and an odd assortment of ornaments collected over the years, each with a story.

That was tradition. That was love—when you cared enough about someone that you wanted to remember everything they gave you.

"They're wonderful." She tried to keep the wobble out of her voice, but her efforts were in vain. Still, she trudged on. "I'm going to have two for breakfast with my coffee."

"Oh, sweetie! Are you crying?"

Eloise blinked back her tears. "I just woke up. My voice is a bit hoarse."

She heard a click, then Olivia's voice came through the phone clearly. She'd taken her off speaker.

"Are you sure you're okay?"

"Yes." She sucked in a breath. "I love the sweater you

bought me. But I wish you hadn't. Laura Beth and I can't afford to exchange gifts. We feel awkward."

"Gifts are gifts, not obligations."

She squeezed her eyes shut, so happy for Olivia that it was hard not to appreciate her gestures. "I know."

"Tucker sent his plane back to New York. He said to get yourself to the airport so you can have Christmas dinner with us."

Eloise pressed her lips together. "Thanks. But I have to work tomorrow, remember? Besides, I'm fine. I'm going to find some Christmas movies on TV and just relax with your mom's cookies."

"Oh, Eloise, come to Kentucky. I can't stand to hear you so sad."

She almost told Olivia that being alone for Christmas wasn't her problem. She almost told her that her heart had finally found a place to rest, but Ricky didn't want her. And that no amount of turkey dinner, Christmas cookies and good friends could make her feel better today.

Instead, she swallowed and said, "I'm fine. I have a new job the first of the year. Just like I told you when you called yesterday, I'm someday going to be a designer."

Olivia's voice brightened. "Yes, you are."

"I'm going to be somebody."

"Yes, you are! Next year you're making all my gowns for the holiday."

"And in a few years, you can help me buy all the art for my penthouse."

Olivia laughed. Eloise smiled. That was what she wanted. To hear Olivia laugh and know she hadn't ruined her Christmas. "Go. Celebrate. I'll be fine."

"Okay. Merry Christmas."

"Merry Christmas."

She clicked off the call and fell back on her pillow. Maybe she could sleep through the day.

Even as the thought crossed her mind, a knock sounded

at her door. Knowing it was probably somebody looking for one of her neighbors, she sighed. Eventually, they'd look at the number on her door, realize their mistake and move on.

They knocked again.

She almost called, "Read the number on my door," but knew they wouldn't hear her from her bedroom. After the third series of knocks, she also realized they weren't going away.

She flipped off her covers, grabbed her fleece robe and scurried to the door, fixing a smile on her face because she truly didn't want to ruin anyone's Christmas. Especially with a scowl over a missed apartment door.

She sucked in a breath, broadened her fake smile and looked through the peephole.

Standing in front of her door and holding a Christmas tree was Norman.

Norman?

She opened the door. "Don't you have family?"

He laughed. "Yes, but I got an entire year's salary to bring this tree to you."

She stepped aside. "That's just crazy."

Ricky walked in behind him. After a quick kiss on her cheek, he said, "I know."

Her heart somersaulted. "What are you doing here?"

He set two bags of ornaments on her sofa. The scent of fresh pine filled the air. He pulled out his cell phone, tapped a few buttons and the music of a carol filled her tiny apartment.

"I'm making your Christmas merry and bright."

Norman tipped his cap. "Unless there's anything else, I'll be going."

Ricky said, "Thanks, Norman."

The driver said, "Merry Christmas," and left.

And then they were alone. Confusion sang through her veins, but so did a sting of pride. No woman wanted to be the charity case of the man she loved. She'd rather be alone than pitied.

She picked up a strand of tinsel. "You didn't have to do this."

"I know."

Pride rose in a fierce roar. "I don't want your charity."

"I know that too."

Frustrated, she made a strangled sound.

"Don't get so huffy. Help me decorate the tree so I can explain."

He held out a shiny blue ball.

With a sigh, she took it.

"Okay, so I went home for the first time in a year and a half."

Although she wanted to be angry, her heart squeezed for him.

"My parents were thrilled to see me. My sisters brought their kids over. My younger brother hugged me."

"Oh. That's so sweet."

"It was."

He said nothing else, just wrapped a strand of lights from the top of the tree, along the branches in circle after circle until he reached the bottom. Then he plugged them in. The tree glowed.

She sighed. "It's beautiful."

"And we're just getting started."

Her heart singing with happiness that would soon become sorrow when he left, she caught his hand. "I can't do this. I can't pretend nothing is wrong. I told you that I loved you and you told me you couldn't love. I accepted that. If you stay, my heart will be broken all over again."

"Even if I tell you that I love you too?"

Her breath froze.

"That's why I'm here." He reached for tinsel and looped it around the fat tree. "I thought I was finally ready to go home. I knew being with you had started to heal me. And

I believed the logical next step was to be with my family."
He faced her and caught her gaze. "Turns out you *had*
helped me heal. Enough, though, that it wasn't my family
I needed. It was you."

"Oh." Her chest had tightened so much that was all she
could say.

He opened his arms. "Come here."

She stepped into them.

"I'm so sorry I hurt you. But I had to go home to realize it was you I needed."

She pulled back. "Say the part about loving me again
and just kiss me."

He laughed. "I love you. Seriously. I fell like a rock."

She smiled, and he kissed her. His lips met hers unerr-
ingly, as if they'd found home, and every cell in her being
rejoiced.

Just then his cell phone blasted the "Hallelujah Chorus."

She would have laughed, except the kiss was too deli-
cious. His lips skimmed across hers, nipped and sipped,
stirring her blood. Her arms lifted slowly, almost as if un-
sure this was real. Her hands walked up his sweater-cov-
ered chest and finally linked behind his neck.

His arms wrapped around her, tightly, securely, as if
he'd never let her go. For the first time in her life, she knew
what it was to be genuinely wanted.

They broke apart slowly, their gazes connected. He
smiled. She smiled.

His whispered words broke the silence. "I never thought
I'd get over my son's death. Then you taught me that you
never get over it, you go on."

She nodded. "It was what I had done with Wayne."

His hand skimmed down her hair. "Have I told you lately
that you're beautiful?"

She laughed. "I don't think you've ever told me I was
beautiful. Your friends have, but you always focused on
my clothes. A nice, safe way to compliment me."

He sniffed a laugh. "No more playing it safe. I want to be in this for everything. The good times and bad."

"That's the way it's supposed to be."

"You agree?"

She nodded.

"Well, since you basically just accepted my marriage proposal—" he took a step back, rummaged through one of the bags "—I guess you'll need this."

He produced a black velvet ring box. Her gaze flew to his. "This is it?"

"This is it."

He got down on one knee, opened the ring box and displayed a huge diamond solitaire. "Will you marry me?"

Her eyes filled with tears. He was the answer to a thousand prayers said on long lonely nights, most of them on Christmases. "Yes!"

He rose and kissed her again. This time she melted. He was the kindest, most wonderful man in the world and now he was hers. She gave herself over to the kiss, opened her mouth, let their tongues twine and dance. As they should because it was the happiest day of her life.

When they finally broke apart, he shifted away. "And there's one more thing."

Through happy tears, Eloise glanced at the second black jeweler's box he handed her. She caught his gaze. "What's this?"

He nudged the box at her. "Open it."

She lifted the lid and an array of diamonds winked at her. She glanced up sharply. "It's a diamond necklace."

"For your mom."

Her brow furrowed. "For my mom?"

"You said the only way you'd ever be accepted into your family would be if you bought your mom a diamond necklace."

She gasped. "I was kidding."

"I thought it through. I think you're right. We need to make a grand gesture to get back into your family."

"If you remember that conversation correctly, I also told you I didn't want to be back with my family."

"Everybody needs family. You'll just go back with new rules. You'll accept what they can give you because you'll have *my* love. You won't ever go without love again. In fact, I'll give you so much you'll have enough left over to give your parents. And eventually, maybe they'll come around. Or maybe they won't. But it won't matter."

She blinked back tears and slid her arms around his neck again. "That's sweet."

"No. That's real love. No family left behind."

She smiled. "*Nobody* left behind."

"Exactly."

This time she kissed him. Long and deep and sweet. And he finally got the chance to do what he'd longed to do for their entire courtship. He let his hand slide from her shoulders, down her long sleek spine, to the swell of her bottom, then back up again.

She was his.

And he was hers.

Neither one of them would ever be alone again on Christmas.

All the dark places in Ricky's heart suddenly lit with glorious light. He'd always miss his son. Always regret his mistakes. But he knew in his heart of hearts, even someone as young as Blake would know everyone deserved a second chance.

He broke the kiss and glanced at the window. Big, fluffy flakes billowed behind the glass. He smiled. "It's snowing."

EPILOGUE

THEY MARRIED A few months later, on a sunny spring day in New York City. Crisp air filled Eloise's lungs as she and Ricky ran out the door of St. Patrick's Cathedral into a sea of bubbles being blown by their guests.

Standing to the right, her mother dabbed tears as her dad straightened to his full six-foot-three, as proud as any father she'd ever seen. Her older brother grinned at her, happy as a clam to be an entrepreneur himself, thanks to an investment by Ricky.

No family left behind.

She still wasn't convinced her parents were as glad to have her back as they were that she was marrying someone with more money than most banks, but as Ricky said, they wouldn't care. Family was family.

With Ricky two steps ahead of her, holding her fingers, she navigated the stairs to the sidewalk in the slim satin gown designed by her boss, Artie Best.

Ricky kissed her knuckles and they ran to the limo, where Norman, in dress blues, awaited them.

He grinned as he opened the door. "I can take you to a hotel for a few hours before the reception."

"Or we can go get the pictures," Eloise said with a laugh.

"Yes, ma'am."

They slid inside, Norman closed the door and Ricky reached for her, giving her a long, slow kiss.

"So, Mrs. Langley, how's it going?"

She laughed. "You just wanted to be the first to call me that."

"I like the sound of it."

"I do too."

"And we're going to be happy together."

"Yes."

She knew it was true because she'd been down this road before. She was smarter now. She hadn't given away her heart willy-nilly, and Ricky hadn't accepted it without thought. This passion would last forever.

Hours later, at the end of the reception, she prepared to toss her bouquet into a throng of hopeful single women. Two seconds before she threw it, she noticed Laura Beth wasn't in the group. She sat at a chair at one of the round tables beside the dance floor.

Seeing this, Eloise was a bit confused as she threw her bouquet, and the bundle of flowers didn't just go too high, it also went too far…

And fell in Laura Beth Matthews's lap.

* * * * *

Mills & Boon® Hardback
November 2014

ROMANCE

A Virgin for His Prize	Lucy Monroe
The Valquez Seduction	Melanie Milburne
Protecting the Desert Princess	Carol Marinelli
One Night with Morelli	Kim Lawrence
To Defy a Sheikh	Maisey Yates
The Russian's Acquisition	Dani Collins
The True King of Dahaar	Tara Pammi
Rebel's Bargain	Annie West
The Million-Dollar Question	Kimberly Lang
Enemies with Benefits	Louisa George
Man vs. Socialite	Charlotte Phillips
Fired by Her Fling	Christy McKellen
The Twelve Dates of Christmas	Susan Meier
At the Chateau for Christmas	Rebecca Winters
A Very Special Holiday Gift	Barbara Hannay
A New Year Marriage Proposal	Kate Hardy
A Little Christmas Magic	Alison Roberts
Christmas with the Maverick Millionaire	Scarlet Wilson

MEDICAL

Playing the Playboy's Sweetheart	Carol Marinelli
Unwrapping Her Italian Doc	Carol Marinelli
A Doctor by Day...	Emily Forbes
Tamed by the Renegade	Emily Forbes

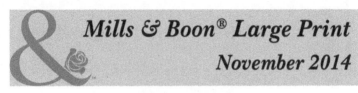

Mills & Boon® Large Print
November 2014

ROMANCE

Christakis's Rebellious Wife	Lynne Graham
At No Man's Command	Melanie Milburne
Carrying the Sheikh's Heir	Lynn Raye Harris
Bound by the Italian's Contract	Janette Kenny
Dante's Unexpected Legacy	Catherine George
A Deal with Demakis	Tara Pammi
The Ultimate Playboy	Maya Blake
Her Irresistible Protector	Michelle Douglas
The Maverick Millionaire	Alison Roberts
The Return of the Rebel	Jennifer Faye
The Tycoon and the Wedding Planner	Kandy Shepherd

HISTORICAL

A Lady of Notoriety	Diane Gaston
The Scarlet Gown	Sarah Mallory
Safe in the Earl's Arms	Liz Tyner
Betrayed, Betrothed and Bedded	Juliet Landon
Castle of the Wolf	Margaret Moore

MEDICAL

200 Harley Street: The Proud Italian	Alison Roberts
200 Harley Street: American Surgeon in London	Lynne Marshall
A Mother's Secret	Scarlet Wilson
Return of Dr Maguire	Judy Campbell
Saving His Little Miracle	Jennifer Taylor
Heatherdale's Shy Nurse	Abigail Gordon

Mills & Boon® Hardback
December 2014

ROMANCE

Taken Over by the Billionaire	Miranda Lee
Christmas in Da Conti's Bed	Sharon Kendrick
His for Revenge	Caitlin Crews
A Rule Worth Breaking	Maggie Cox
What The Greek Wants Most	Maya Blake
The Magnate's Manifesto	Jennifer Hayward
To Claim His Heir by Christmas	Victoria Parker
Heiress's Defiance	Lynn Raye Harris
Nine Month Countdown	Leah Ashton
Bridesmaid with Attitude	Christy McKellen
An Offer She Can't Refuse	Shoma Narayanan
Breaking the Boss's Rules	Nina Milne
Snowbound Surprise for the Billionaire	Michelle Douglas
Christmas Where They Belong	Marion Lennox
Meet Me Under the Mistletoe	Cara Colter
A Diamond in Her Stocking	Kandy Shepherd
Falling for Dr December	Susanne Hampton
Snowbound with the Surgeon	Annie Claydon

MEDICAL

Midwife's Christmas Proposal	Fiona McArthur
Midwife's Mistletoe Baby	Fiona McArthur
A Baby on Her Christmas List	Louisa George
A Family This Christmas	Sue MacKay

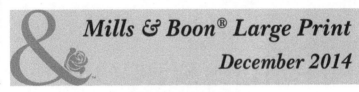

Mills & Boon® Large Print
December 2014

ROMANCE

Zarif's Convenient Queen	Lynne Graham
Uncovering Her Nine Month Secret	Jennie Lucas
His Forbidden Diamond	Susan Stephens
Undone by the Sultan's Touch	Caitlin Crews
The Argentinian's Demand	Cathy Williams
Taming the Notorious Sicilian	Michelle Smart
The Ultimate Seduction	Dani Collins
The Rebel and the Heiress	Michelle Douglas
Not Just a Convenient Marriage	Lucy Gordon
A Groom Worth Waiting For	Sophie Pembroke
Crown Prince, Pregnant Bride	Kate Hardy

HISTORICAL

Beguiled by Her Betrayer	Louise Allen
The Rake's Ruined Lady	Mary Brendan
The Viscount's Frozen Heart	Elizabeth Beacon
Mary and the Marquis	Janice Preston
Templar Knight, Forbidden Bride	Lynna Banning

MEDICAL

200 Harley Street: The Soldier Prince	Kate Hardy
200 Harley Street: The Enigmatic Surgeon	Annie Claydon
A Father for Her Baby	Sue MacKay
The Midwife's Son	Sue MacKay
Back in Her Husband's Arms	Susanne Hampton
Wedding at Sunday Creek	Leah Martyn

MILLS & BOON®

Why shop at millsandboon.co.uk?

Each year, thousands of romance readers find their perfect read at millsandboon.co.uk. That's because we're passionate about bringing you the very best romantic fiction. Here are some of the advantages of shopping at www.millsandboon.co.uk:

* **Get new books first**—you'll be able to buy your favourite books one month before they hit the shops

* **Get exclusive discounts**—you'll also be able to buy our specially created monthly collections, with up to 50% off the RRP

* **Find your favourite authors**—latest news, interviews and new releases for all your favourite authors and series on our website, plus ideas for what to try next

* **Join in**—once you've bought your favourite books, don't forget to register with us to rate, review and join in the discussions

Visit **www.millsandboon.co.uk**
for all this and more today!